THE GIRL CHASE

Whilst Dale Shand is on a 'private business' trip in Los Angeles, he witnesses a gun killing. Shand soon becomes caught up in a series of adventures, which sweep through Old Mexico to New York — with torrid sequences in Arizona, Nevada and Chicago along the way ... He encounters gorgeous girls, sinister men, and the eccentric and indestructible Ma McGarritty. For the first time in his career, Shand finds himself both the hunter and the hunted.

DOUGLAS ENEFER

THE GIRL CHASE

Complete and Unabridged

LINFORD
Leicester

First published in Great Britain by
Robert Hale Limited
London

First Linford Edition
published 2006
by arrangement with
Robert Hale Limited
London

British Library CIP Data

Enefer, Douglas
    The girl chase.—Large print ed.—
Linford mystery library
    1. Suspense fiction
    2. Large type books
    I. Title
    823.9'14 [F]

    ISBN 1–84617–334–5

Published by
F. A. Thorpe (Publishing)
Anstey, Leicestershire

Set by Words & Graphics Ltd.
Anstey, Leicestershire
Printed and bound in Great Britain by
T. J. International Ltd., Padstow, Cornwall

This book is printed on acid-free paper

To BERT WARD . . . who set
the idea going

1

I was sitting on a high stool against a long, narrow bar on The Strip when she came in, wedged herself next to me and ordered brandy. Her voice was husky, with a small abrasive edge to it, like a drinker's voice.

'It's gone a little cool outside, hasn't it?' she said.

I half turned to see her. She was in her mid-thirties and must have been a very handsome girl before the hard liquor got her. Even now, with a small sag under the chin and lines fanning out from her eyes, she still had looks. But they were running to shabbiness, like the crumpled black dress she was wearing. It was a used face, a face which had seen too much of the wrong kind of living; but not a beaten face. The widely-set blue eyes looked out with a sort of defiant candour.

'Yeah,' I said, 'it's cool.' In fact, I hadn't

really noticed it because I live in New York and this was Southern California. I was in Los Angeles on some small private business and was going back in the morning. I wondered if she was trying to make a pitch, but her next words didn't suggest it.

'It's so much warmer in Pasadena,' she mused. 'I wish I'd never left it.' She drank some of the brandy and went on. 'You're not in the show business, by any chance?'

'No, why?'

She lit a cigarette with a book match, blew it out and said: 'Sometimes show business people come in here. Not that it makes any difference.'

'Any difference to what or to whom?'

'Forget it,' she shrugged. She put the rest of her drink down in a lump and bought another. I looked at her again and had a sudden impression that I had seen her face before somewhere, perhaps a long time ago. I tried to recall the circumstances, but nothing surfaced. She put a folded five dollar bill on the bar and began humming to herself, a snatch from an old number Peggy Lee used to sing.

She was moving off the melodic line into an improvisation when I remembered the title.

'I know that one,' I said, 'it's *Let's Call It a Day* . . . '

She broke off with a short laugh, a laugh emptied of humour. 'Yes, that's right,' she answered. 'Very appropriate.'

'For you, you mean?'

'I'd like to think otherwise, but I guess it fits.' She gave me a long, level look, full-faced, and suddenly I knew who she was.

'Annette Falaise,' I said. 'That's who you are, isn't it?'

For a long moment she didn't answer. Then she put a hand out, and touched my sleeve. 'Bless you,' she said. 'For remembering, I mean . . . '

I hadn't seen her in a decade. The last time was in the Stardust Room of the Statton House on Fifth Avenue. The vanished memory crystallized in my mind, making a picture of an arresting dark-haired girl sheathed in diamanté-studded white standing in the spotlight and singing the agreeable sweet nothings

3

of George Gershwin and the sophisticated disenchantment of Cole Porter in a warm, vibrant contralto laced with acquired inflexions of the blues. Annette Falaise . . . a singer with the undying durability of the great practitioners in the trade. And then, suddenly, she wasn't around any more.

She had walked out in the middle of a three-week season in Las Vegas and married Dino Carelli and nobody sued for breach of contract on account of Dino owned a piece of the gambling place where she sang and wasn't the kind of fellow whose girl it was policy to sue if you didn't want to wear lead next to the skin. For a while the disc jockeys went on spinning her old records; then a new race of singers mushroomed on the socked-out beat of the three-chord guitar bashers and unsold pressings of *Annette Falaise Sings the All-Time Hits* gathered dust, and stayed unsold. For her an epoch had ended even before it attained its peak.

'Bless you for remembering,' she said again. 'You're the first man to do that in a long time.'

'You shouldn't have quit,' I said. 'You had something — the timeless thing that makes for greatness.'

'Yes.' She said it in a low, meditative voice. Then she looked up and added bitterly: 'I still have it . . . I can still sing . . . '

I thought of the hummed improvisation. It had sounded acutely professional, but maybe a voice coarsened by drink wouldn't stand a sustained effort now. And she couldn't face the pitiless lights any more.

She made another laugh. 'I know exactly what you're thinking,' she said. 'You think my voice is probably loused-up with booze, that my clothes were bought the year before last and that I haven't kept my looks. Check.'

'I'll always think of you as one of the great classic pop singers, Miss Falaise,' I said.

'Yes, like I belong in the past tense,' she replied. 'Well, I'm only thirty-four and I can still do it if they'd give me even one break. Just one break is all I want to get off the hard stuff, slim down a little and put myself in the right clothes and . . . '

She bit on her underlip and I said, just to be saying something — anything: 'They don't want to know, the guys in the business, is that it?'

'I've knocked on so many doors,' she said. 'The managers, the agents, the A and R men. Some of them don't even remember me from when. And those who do aren't interested, except the ones who undress you with their eyes and have trouble with their hands.'

'I'm sorry.' I looked at her glass. It was empty. I signalled the white-jacketed bartender with my eyes and he set up another for her.

'Thanks,' she said. 'Though I drink too much. I drink because I'm unhappy and I'm unhappy because I drink. There's no way out.' She looked at me with a quick smile. 'I'm washed-up and I know it, but I keep kidding myself there'll be just one more chance. Is that bad?'

'Not if you fight back hard enough to change it into reality.'

'I've tried, but maybe not hard enough or often enough. You get tired of butting a stone wall . . . and all the humiliations that go with this business when you've been big and are on the skids.'

There didn't seem to be anything to say and I was wondering how to get out without hurting her when she said, 'I guess I get by all right. I've a place to live, food to eat and enough money to drink with. It's too late really to climb back.'

'I suppose so, Miss Falaise.'

'That's not my real name, you know,' she said. Her voice was thickening, she was starting to get stoned. 'It's Maisie Toblatt. I invented Annette Falaise out of something I once read in a French magazine. I haven't been in L.A. long. I'm living with a man who runs a souvenir store for tourists. He's past sixty, so he doesn't make demands on me, only about once in a month.' She put her glass down and went on, 'I've been drinking all day since about eleven this morning. You're a nice guy. I like you. What's your name?'

'Dale Shand.'

'And you're not in this dirty, stinking business?'

'No.' I didn't tell her what kind of dirty business I was in.

'I shouldn't have married Dino,' she said inconsequentially.

'Dino Carelli, wasn't it?'

'Yes. The great Dino. The great, four-flushing Dino Carelli. And I fell for *that* . . . '

'What happened to him?'

'He found a new baby,' she said. She seemed fond of fitting song titles into her conversation. 'Then he got shot down by the police in a bank heist. I heard he was in the prison hospital the first three months. I never saw him again.'

'I'm sorry.'

'Forget it, Mr. Shand. Let's have another li'l drink and . . . ' She stopped abruptly. She was looking in the long mirror behind the massed bottles in the back of the bar, her face suddenly frozen. A man was coming across the floor, a loose shambling man wearing a navy mohair suit with his tie pulled down from an unbuttoned shirt collar; a man with a pallor on the hard tight skin of a face that looked as if it had once been boldly handsome.

He moved out of vision up to the other end of the bar, tossed money on the counter and said: 'Whisky sour.' He hadn't seen us, he wasn't even looking in the same direction. I had an odd prickly sensation; I knew, without waiting for her to tell me, who he was.

'Dino . . . ' She said the name in a rustle of barely audible sound.

'He hasn't seen you,' I said. 'Maybe he wouldn't recognize you anyway after all these years. Do you want to slip out without him noticing?'

'Please . . . '

'There's a rear exit. Just get off your stool and walk down the bar to the other end. He'll never know.'

'Thank you,' she said.

She slid her feet to the floor and had started down the dimly-lit bar when the street door burst open and a fat smiling man came down the steps. He had three chins on a face like stale lard, but he didn't look soft. IIe made a small dissonance of laughter and his right hand swept inside his loose jacket. The bartender stood transfixed, a glass in one hand, a polishing cloth in the other. Annette Falaise had gone.

The shambling man who was Dino Carelli had swivelled completely round on his stool. His hand must have moved, too, but I didn't see it happen.

'I can fade that any time,' he said. He had already triggered a nine-shot Colt, .43 calibre. The big slug hit the fat man straight between the eyes and he was dead when he put his face in the floor.

2

I didn't move. The bartender didn't move. He was still transfixed in his last attitude. Dino Carelli, no longer shambling, backed off from the bar. He was aiming the Colt from just above the hip.

'Freeze the hands on the bar,' he said. 'Don't nobody get any fancy ideas.'

I turned. That made me see eye to eye with the bartender. Sweat was running down his boyish face. I wasn't feeling much better; I had my back to the gun.

Carelli said suddenly: 'I thought there was a broad in here. I'm not sure, but I thought there was one.'

'There was,' I croaked.

'I didn't see her, you being in the way and the lousy lighting in here. Where is she?'

'She left.'

'I didn't see her go.'

'She went just before it happened. She used the rear exit.'

Carelli made a small sound that could be a laugh, or not. 'So she wasn't an eye-witness,' he said. 'But you two guys saw me give it to him. That's bad . . . '

The way he stopped speaking was too sudden and the sweat crawled down my spine like melted ice.

'Yeah,' he said carefully, 'that's bad. You might get ideas about talking to the johns. I got to block that play is all.'

I dropped straight down to the floor as he fired. The bullet shattered the mirror behind the counter. There was no sign of the boyish bartender; he must have been on the floor, too. I rolled fast behind a table, pulled it down like a shield as footsteps sounded on the stairs.

Dino Carelli jumped sideways as three men strolled in, then rushed up the steps to the sidewalk. I threw the table over and went after him, but when I got there he had vanished. I went back into the bar. The three men were shouting incoherent questions. The boyish bartender rose into view, splaying both hands on the counter. They were shaking, out of control. I grabbed the telephone and called Central Homicide.

The dead man was spreadeagled on the floor as if he had been nailed to it. His hat had fallen off and his brown hair sloped grotesquely. It wasn't his hair.

I poured a stiff brandy and handed the glass to the bartender. He had to use both hands to stop it rattling against his teeth. One of the three men, a big man with a face like an agitated horse, bawled: 'Say, what's going on . . . '

I looked down at the figure on the floor. 'He went for a gun, but the fellow who just left beat him to it,' I said.

The horse-faced man sagged and said: 'I don't want any part of this, I'm getting out of . . . '

'You're too late,' I said. Sirens were wailing out on the street and in another moment booted feet thudded down the steps. They belonged to a couple of bluecoats, a youngish one with a pale eager face and a middle-aged cop with spiky grey hair and a coarsened reddish skin.

He stared down at the body, moved it slightly with his foot and said: 'What gives? Talk it up and make it fast.'

'I came down here for a drink,' I said. 'While I was having it a man came and sat at the other end of the bar. Then this fat guy walked in and reached inside his jacket, very fast. Only not quite so fast as the man at the end of the bar.'

'You mean the fellow sitting at the bar shot him?'

'Once, between the eyes.'

'Why?'

'I imagine they had reasons for wanting to kill each other, but as I never saw either of them before in my life I don't have any idea what the reasons could be,' I said.

The coarse skin flushed a darker red. He looked as if he suspected insult but was unable to pin it down. 'Yeah? Well, don't crack wise with me,' he said.

'I'm not. I'm telling you what happened and exactly how it happened. I assume you want to know that.'

'Yeah, I want to know. When this guy on the floor got dead what happened next?'

'The killer went out of the bar, officer.'

'You didn't try to stop him?'

'He had a gun,' I said patiently. 'He was going to kill both the bartender and myself. In fact, he fired at me, only I had guessed his intention and dropped to the floor. Then these three fellows came in and he ran past them up the steps. When I got to the street there was no sign of him.'

The boy behind the bar said in a flat voice full of quiet shock, 'That's just how it happened, just like that.'

The middle-aged cop went down on one knee and turned the dead man over. The younger one said uncertainly: 'We hadn't ought to touch him until the captain of detectives arrives.'

'We ain't moved him, Charley. We just took a look to see if we knew him, that's what we did.'

'The captain mightn't like it,' Charley objected.

'The hell with what he don't . . . ' The older bluecoat stopped suddenly as two men came down into the bar. A tall man in a grey suit with clear blue eyes in a composed face accompanied by a slightly less tall man wearing a brown checked jacket and light cavalry twill slacks.

The tall man looked carefully at the body, then looked carefully from one face to another. 'Well?' he said. His voice, like his movements, seemed slow; the deceptive slowness of a man who would reach an objective a good deal faster than most.

Charley, the young bluecoat, said quickly: 'We were going south on Sunset when we picked up the message on the prowl car radio and came here a few minutes ago.'

'I see. Which of you called us on the phone?'

'I did.' I stepped forward.

The tall man said: 'Logan, captain of detectives, Central Homicide. This is Detective-lieutenant Hammer. Your name, address and occupation, please.'

I told them. Twin lines forked above the bridge of Hammer's sharp nose. 'A private dick,' he said. 'That New York licence don't buy you anything out here.'

'I'm not trying to buy anything,' I said. 'I'm not here in a professional capacity. I came here to attend to some small private business and happened to witness a murder.' I repeated what I had already told the two bluecoats and went on, 'I should explain that while I was having the drink I had some conversation with a woman who used to be a singer named Annette Falaise. When the first man came in she saw his reflection in the mirror and said he was her ex-husband and that she hadn't seen him in years and didn't want to see him now. At least, that's what she conveyed. She said his name was Dino Carelli.'

The middle-aged cop's face was dark with blood. 'You never said anything about that,' he whispered.

'I'm saying it now,' I answered. 'Does the name mean anything to you, captain?'

Logan nodded. 'Yeah, though he wasn't convicted here and, so far as we know, never lived here. It was in San Francisco, a bank heist.'

'That's what Annette Falaise told me. She said the police shot him, that he spent some time in hospital and that she never saw him again.'

'And Carelli walked in here and didn't recognize her?'

'I don't believe he saw her. He just had a vague impression there was a woman in here, that's all. The lighting is dim where we sat and I was in his line of vision, even supposing he was looking. In point of fact, he wasn't. He just sat up at the other end of the bar nursing a drink and not looking in any particular direction, unless it was at the stairs.'

'You mean he was or was not expecting this other guy and was or was not looking for him?' asked Logan.

'I was just airing a possibility, captain. Frankly, I don't know.'

Hammer made a harsh sound. 'We'll do any theorizing that's called for,' he sneered. 'You stick to the facts. Maybe Carelli don't see this broad, but he could hear her voice, couldn't he?'

'After he came in she barely spoke, and then only in an undertone.' I thought for a moment and said, 'Do you think there's a lead in the fact that she was once his wife?'

Logan shrugged. 'Could be there's a

18

connection. On the other hand, perhaps not. The way you tell it, there doesn't appear to have been any arrangement for them to meet here. You say she was gone before he pulled a gun?'

'Yes. She didn't want to see him — or, more accurately, she didn't want him to see her.'

'Well, maybe it doesn't have any significance. Only she could have told us things.'

'About Dino Carelli?'

'Possibly, though if she hasn't seen him in years it mightn't have added up to anything. Just the same, I'd like to talk with her. I suppose she didn't tell you her address?'

'No, but she said she was living with a man who owns a small souvenir store here, a man in his sixties. That ought to help.'

'It's enough to trace her,' replied Logan.

Hammer made a balled fist, looked at it, then unwound the fingers. 'You took your time telling us that, pal,' he said softly.

'We've only been talking about ten minutes, lieutenant. I don't think she'll have run away.'

'Any other little thing you just thought of or don't want to tell?' said Hammer tightly. He took a cigarette from a crumpled pack, put it between his teeth unlit. 'We don't want a shamus from New York trying to do our work for us,' he added.

Logan said quietly, 'So far as it goes, Shand seems to have acted correctly. He witnessed a murder, tried to follow the killer, called Headquarters and has given us his story.'

'He could be holding something back just to get himself a big play in the newspapers, captain.'

'I doubt if he'd like that kind of publicity,' answered Logan dryly.

'Prospective clients wouldn't like it, which is more to the point,' I grunted. 'Nobody wants to hire a private investigator who gets headline quotes in a murder case.'

'That's true. On the other hand, you might have another reason for holding something back.'

'I might — if I had a client to protect. In point of fact, I haven't had one in three and a half weeks.'

'You're breaking my heart,' grinned Hammer.

Logan said directly, 'Are you holding anything back?'

I shook my head as the police doctor arrived, followed immediately by the fingerprint experts and a uniformed man with a Leica and flash gear. They were all busy as bees when the ambulance crew showed up with a Neilson stretcher.

I said to Logan, 'Do you want me to make a sworn statement, captain?'

'Not immediately — later. We'll locate Annette Falaise and try to find out why Carelli was in L.A.'

'I've just remembered one other thing,' I said. 'It's only small, but you'd better know. Annette Falaise said she came here fairly recently, I think, from Pasadena.'

Hammer showed me his tight face again. 'You keep remembering things, don't you?'

'I don't think there's anything else,

lieutenant,' I said mildly.

The middle-aged bluecoat, who had been going through the dead man's pockets, looked up and said bleakly, 'Nothing on him, captain — not a thing which clues his identity. No social security card, no business card, nothing . . . except this.' He held up a crocodile-skin billfold.

Logan took it from him and got it open. It was jammed with money, mostly hundred dollar bills. He pursed his lips slightly and said, 'Anything else?'

Charley, who had been poking a hand in the dead man's shirt pocket, said: 'One cigarette . . .'

The captain held it under his nose and sniffed. 'Marijuana, I think.'

'So the guy was a viper,' said Hammer. He shrugged. 'Not that it gets us anywhere.'

'You never can tell,' replied Logan. He turned to me and said, 'How long did you say you were staying in L.A., Mr. Shand?'

'I didn't, but as a matter of fact I have a reservation on the nine a.m. flight tomorrow.'

The ambulance crew got the body on the stretcher and covered it. Logan nodded to them, then said equably, 'I'm afraid you won't be able to catch that flight, Mr. Shand. You'd better come downtown a little later and make that statement. Where are you staying?'

I told him the hotel and he said, 'You won't be able to leave Los Angeles without permission, but we won't withhold that after the coroner's inquiry.'

'I understand, captain.'

He nodded. Then, quite suddenly, he held out a hand. 'Thanks for your help,' he said. 'I liked the way you gave us the facts.'

I went out of the bar. A chill, damp mist was drifting in from the Pacific. Soon it would have merged with a million grimy particles to make a Los Angeles smog. I mingled with the drifting crowds on the sidewalk, going north towards Sunset and Vine. Sleek, fat cars with faces like grinning sharks went by with their headlights on. I was almost at the intersection when one of them, a shining black Lincoln, slid to a halt alongside me.

The driver, a boy with a pale expressionless face, thrust a hand through the wound-down window and opened the rear door. From the darkened interior a voice said: 'You cannot see it, but a gun is looking at you . . . please step inside.'

I looked quickly at the open door; maybe I could slam it shut. Without turning his pale face the driver, who was sitting with a foot on the clutch and the motor idling, said: 'I wouldn't try anything, if I was you. He's holding a Luger. It'd blow a hole in you big enough to drive a Greyhound bus through . . . '

I got in the car, the driver let his clutch in and nosed out into the traffic stream. The smog was coming down now, but he drove calmly as if he hadn't a care in the world. Unlike Shand.

3

The man sitting carefully in the padded rear of the car with me might have been a banker, except that bankers rarely issue invitations at the point of a gun. He had a long face and long exquisitely-manicured hands one of which was holding the Luger hard down on his beautifully-tailored thigh with the muzzle not more than six inches from me. He wore a flat grey suit and a flat white shirt with a buttoned-down collar. His sole concession to ostentation was a gold tiepin which carried a single diamond not quite so powerful as a blow-torch.

'You were observed leaving the bar,' he said. 'Some information is required from you.'

'Why couldn't you have just pulled-in and asked me without the melodrama?'

He smiled, a long brilliant smile full of nothing. 'You might not have been willing. It was necessary to make quite

25

sure. Then again, a lengthy interrogation is scarcely feasible in so public a place as Sunset Boulevard.'

'I see. Can I smoke?'

He held out a gold cigarette case. He put the case away and snapped a matching gold lighter alive. 'I prefer that you do not put your hands other than where they can be seen,' he said.

I dragged on the cigarette and looked through the window. The smog had thinned a little and the car was climbing now. Opulent homes, all pastel-washed stucco and terra cotta tiles, swam into view beyond broad lawns and sweeping driveways flanked by flowering trees and shrubs. The houses looked down on the road as if with the unconscious arrogance of wealth. Most of them were tilted up the lower slopes of the Santa Monica Mountains separating Los Angeles from the San Fernando Valley. That meant we were in Beverly Hills.

The man with the long face said, 'You will please place this over your eyes.' It was a strip of black velvet with tapered ends so that you could tie them.

'You came prepared, didn't you?' I said.

'Not specifically. It has been used on other occasions and I chanced to have it in the car. Kindly place it in position immediately.'

I did what he said; there wasn't anything else I could do. I wondered who they were; I already had a firm idea about why they wanted to interrogate me. A plan had gone wrong and they wanted to know how and why and where Carelli had gone. As if I knew.

The car went on climbing, then made a slow left turn. Gravel crunched under the tyres. That meant we were on a private driveway. The motor stopped, the driver pulled his handbrake up against the rachet and we got out. The Luger was in the small of my back.

The long-faced man said, 'Just walk straight ahead, please.'

I walked across some more gravel with him behind me, then up six steps and into a house. The door closed behind us with a heavy click.

'You can remove the strip now,' he said.

I pulled it off and stared around. We

were in a vast domed hallway with a tiled floor. There was a musicians' gallery high up on the wall to my right, and below it a line of figures in chain armour; the leading one looked about ready to charge.

The gun stabbed into my spine again and I went through a brass-studded door into a room not quite so large as Grand Central Station. It was a fair sample of Beverly Hills baronial style — a shaggy white wall-to-wall carpet, vivid crimson upholstery, refrectory table, English oak panelling, an open brick fireplace big enough to roast a buffalo if we still had any buffaloes, a palm tree growing straight up towards the distant ceiling, a curved bar for cocktails and a six-string Spanish guitar for strumming if the hi-fi radio-phonograph went on the blink.

The room was empty.

'Perhaps you would like a drink?' the man with the Luger pistol suggested. 'Please help yourself — whisky, gin, cognac, vodka, whichever you prefer. The Scotch is wholly admirable. By the way, you didn't mention your name.'

'You didn't ask me,' I said.

He smiled his long smile again. It was still loaded with nothing. 'The asking will begin very shortly,' he said.

I poured myself about three fingers of Scotch from a cut-glass decanter which could have been a collector's piece. The superbly-tailored man sank back in one of the crimson chairs with his gun still hard down on a thigh. He had the air of a man who knows he is on the verge of being entertained.

I drank some of my drink. It was Scotch all right. You could almost smell the Highland heather and hear the skirl of the pipes in the misted glen. What I actually heard was a flat, expressionless voice, slightly amplified and all-encompassing because it was being piped into the enormous room through stereophonic loudspeakers.

'I prefer to speak to you unseen, though I am able to observe you quite clearly over closed circuit television. I have already been informed of the circumstances under which you have been brought here. You will answer some questions — truthfully if you desire to avoid the disagreeable consequences of falsehood or evasion. First, your name.'

I told him. There didn't seem to be anything to lose by not telling him. Except most likely my life.

'Your place of residence and your occupation, please.'

'New York. I'm a private investigator by trade.'

The long-featured man with the long gun sat upright rather suddenly. His curiously brilliant eyes had a look in them I didn't particularly like.

'A private investigator?' The unseen speaker let his voice descend to a gentle purr. 'This exceptionally monied town, Mr. Shand, already has thirty-four private detective agencies. There would seem to be little scope here for a single operator from New York.'

'At the last count Beverly Hills had nearly two thousand swimming pools and getting along for a couple of hundred psychiatrists, but I guess there's always room for one more,' I said.

The flat voice took on a discernible

edge. 'State your business in Los Angeles, Mr. Shand.'

I drank some more of the whisky, not speaking.

The voice went on, 'You have the look of a courageous man, *amico*, but in the special circumstances in which you find yourself courage is not enough. We have methods of persuasion which have reduced brave men to screaming disintegration. Please do not force us to use them.'

I set the glass down on a beaten-copper side table and said: 'I came to Los Angeles to wind up some minor private business, nothing to do with any sort of investigation. I was intending to return to New York on the early morning flight. I went into the bar for a drink and saw one man kill another man. I had never previously seen either of them. The man who did the killing made his getaway. I called the police and told them what I saw.'

'And you had no connection of any kind with this killer?'

'I've already said as much. I can't make

you believe that if you've already made up your mind.'

'I never make up my mind on the basis of preconceptions or emotional prejudices, Mr. Shand. Only facts interest me. I think you are telling the facts . . . but not all of them. You will be well advised not to keep anything back. A man has been killed, a man who was a subordinate but nevertheless a trusted executive of ours . . . '

'You mean he was a hired gunman who got beaten to the draw,' I sneered.

The man in the crimson chair jutted the Luger out, aiming at my stomach. The disembodied voice chuckled.

'Frank is getting a little impatient, *amico*. It would be prudent not to test him too much . . . better for you, eh? Now listen, Mr. Shand. You were seen to enter the bar. You were followed almost immediately by a woman, a former singer whose professional name is Annette Falaise. She is the legal wife of the man who killed our friend, a man called Dino Carelli. It is possible that you had some conversation with her . . . '

I didn't answer in words, but perhaps something in my expression did. The unseen man said suavely, 'I think she spoke to you, Mr. Shand. She is a woman who would do just that. It is imperative that we establish contact with her.'

'You want to find Carelli and you think she can tell you where he's likely to be?' I said.

'How admirably you put it, Mr. Shand.'

'And you think I may know where she lives?'

'Do you?'

'She didn't tell me her address — we weren't that intimate. She saw Carelli's reflection in a mirror behind the bar as he came in. He didn't see her because he sat at the other end and I was blocking his line of vision. She didn't want him to see her and at my suggestion she slipped out by the rear exit while I covered her.'

'That was most considerate of you, *amico*. And her address?'

'I told you, she didn't give me her address.'

'An indication, perhaps?'

'She said she came from Pasadena and

was living with an elderly man who ran some kind of store. But you're too late. I told the police that much and by now they'll likely have found her.'

'The coppers — bah! A storekeeper, an elderly storekeeper . . . we shall find him . . . and then we shall speak to the Signora Carelli.' Another chuckle came through the stereo speakers. 'The coppers cannot keep her in custody, they have no reason to since she can tell them nothing about the shooting. But we have other questions to ask, and so we have the long talk with her . . . most persuasive . . . '

Suddenly, in that warm room I felt cold. I heard myself saying loudly, 'She hasn't seen Carelli since he went to the pen. She can't tell you anything.'

'She was his wife, she knows his habits, his friends, his interests. Be assured that she will have much to tell us, Mr. Shand. And now, with our thanks for your co-operation, you are free to go.'

Frank stood up. His long face showed nothing. 'We can go out through the french windows,' he said. 'I'll have Al drive you back to L.A.'

I walked across the shaggy white pile, almost dragging my feet. Even a few seconds gained might help, though it seemed like the longest chance. Neither Al nor anyone else was going to drive me back to Los Angeles. If they did I would go to the police and Annette Falaise would be held in protective custody.

The french windows were closed, but as I neared them there was a faint metallic sound and they opened outwards. I stepped out into a Japanese garden, massed with plastic white hyacinths.

'Straight on, Mr. Shand,' said Frank.

Behind us in the enormous room the stereophonic voice said gently, 'Farewell, amico . . .'

Ahead of me a miniature arched bridge crossed an artificial stream which meandered nowhere in particular. I dragged myself on to it. Something moved in the bushes beyond the bridge. I dived headlong to the hump-backed floor as the hail of bullets blasted above me. Then I was twisting sideways and crashing through the slim rails. The stream was about four feet deep. I went down to the bottom, surfaced through a mass of tangled rushes behind a huge, partly-submerged rock.

I could hear Frank yelling up on the bridge. 'You stay there, Al . . . I'm going back into the house for a searchlight . . . we got to find him . . . '

He went away and the machine-gunner stepped out from the bushes, moving very carefully and swinging the gun in a wide, slow arc. The fog was coming down again, but I could see him without being seen. I was down behind the rock on my knees with the water up to my neck. I reached for a stone and tossed it into the stream, away from me. It made a small plop and he reacted at once, swinging the sub-machine gun outwards.

I had no more than seconds in which to act, for he was only a few feet from me. I hurled myself up the small bank. He heard the sound and wheeled, but he was too late. My head rammed his belly and he shot straight backwards into the bushes. I grabbed the fallen machine gun and swung it down on him as he jumped up with a flick-knife. The heavy stock hit the side of his head and he went down as if he had been poleaxed.

Frank was back on the bridge, with the white-featured boy who drove the Lincoln. They had a searchlight focused.

I turned the sub-machine gun and squeezed the trigger. The bullets tore into the lamp.

'Don't go back in the house and don't try anything or you both get the next burst,' I snarled. There was a path going diagonally through the bushes. I ran along it. The path merged with the gravel driveway. The parked Lincoln was on it. I had yanked the door open when shouts and footsteps sounded inside the house.

I raked the main entrance with a long burst and slid down behind the steering wheel. The key was in the ignition. I gunned the motor in second, swung the car out on to the road and shifted into top. The fog had thinned again and I sent the speedometer needle into the high eighties and held it there. I knew they would come after me, but I had a long enough start.

Long enough to abandon the car when I came down into the inner suburbs of L.A. I flagged a cruising taxi and rode to my hotel. I had changed my drenched clothes when the telephone rang. It was Logan, the captain of detectives.

'I thought you were coming downtown to sign a statement,' he began.

'I'm coming now, captain . . . I have something to tell you.'

'Oh?' There was a small gritty edge to his voice.

'It isn't something I omitted, captain. It's something that's just happened. Did you find out where Annette Falaise lives?'

'Yeah, we found the place — but she's blown. The guy she's been living with says she came back in a disturbed condition, packed a bag and went. He doesn't know where she's gone.'

4

I made a small sound and Logan said interestedly: 'What's on your mind?'

When I told him he answered in his calm voice: 'A gang killing. We don't have any information about a gang holed-up in Beverly Hills. Can you name the house you were taken to?'

'No. I could find it again, though.'

'All right. Did they follow you back to L.A.?'

'I don't know, captain. If they did I didn't see them, but I had a start.'

'So you just said. Did you get the car's registration number, by any chance?'

'I'm sorry, no. I was rather preoccupied with a desire to make a getaway. I imagine I was breaking every speed ordinance you have around here. I'd have been glad to see a motorcycle cop.'

'No doubt. Anything else?'

'One thing, yes. These men, whoever

they are, will try to contact Annette Falaise.'

'I'm expecting Hammer back in a few minutes, not much longer. I'll have him look in on that store again with a couple of uniformed men.'

'You traced it quickly.'

'Yeah. An elderly party named Luke Elman runs the place. It's on Bricker Avenue — close to your hotel, as a matter of fact.'

'And she didn't say where she was going?'

'I told you that. She just said she was going away for a short while. So far as you're concerned, you'd better come down to Headquarters right away.'

I hung up and went from the room, but not immediately downtown. Bricker Avenue was close at hand, he had said. I had a sudden unbidden urge to get there ahead of Hammer. Unbidden and irrational because I wasn't on a case, or was I? If I was it wouldn't even pay the cab fare.

I got there inside five minutes. It was a small double-fronted store with a plate-glass door. On the glass in cursive black script was his name. Nothing else. The windows on either side of the double door were strewn with tourist junk, maps of Beverly Hills and brochures stuffed with information about the homes of Hollywood motion picture stars.

There were no customers inside, only Luke Elman. He looked a sprightly sixty — slim, sun-tanned and bright-eyed behind oval spectacles with gold rims. He wore a navy blue shirt outside white cotton slacks. His hair was thinning and was grey almost to the point of being bleached.

He looked up inquiringly from behind the cash register as I tramped in, and said: 'Good evening, sir. Can I help you?'

'It's possible, Mr. Elman, if not probable.'

'I beg your pardon.' His voice, which was a little high-pitched, sounded startled.

I said: 'My name is Dale Shand. I had a conversation with Miss Falaise in a bar ... ' I paused because of the expression which had moved on his face and went on: 'It's not what you may be thinking. I'd better explain.'

When I was through he said uneasily: 'I don't like all this. I don't want to be mixed-up in it.'

'That's understandable, Mr. Elman. But it's more than possible that she may be in some personal danger. Because of that and for no other reason I'd like to contact her quickly.'

He twitched the gold-rimmed glasses off his nose and began polishing them agitatedly. 'I told the police that I didn't know where Annette had gone. I can't add to that, Mr. Shand.'

'I see. Suppose we try it another way?'

'I . . . I don't quite understand.'

'Apart from yourself, has she any friends — anyone to whom she might have confided?'

He put the glasses back on his face and blinked through them. 'Now you mention it, she does have a friend here. A girl, a girl named Julie Arden.'

It was a long chance, but it might be worth following up. I said: 'Do you know where Miss Arden lives?'

'Why, yes. She has an apartment not far from here. It's on a little street, La Jaquita

Crescent, off Ventura.' His eyes jumped. 'Do you think Annette may be there?'

'I don't know what to think, Mr. Elman, except that I'd better find out.'

He turned a worn signet ring on the third finger of his left hand, looked up and said: 'Danger, you say? You don't mean . . . '

'The men who kidnapped me want to talk to her, Mr. Elman. They're dangerous people. I just think she ought to be warned. More than that, I think she had better go to the police for protection.'

He shivered. 'Annette wasn't always easy to live with,' he said. 'She was an unhappy person, unhappy deep down inside. But I'm terribly fond of her. My God . . . if anything happened to her I don't know what I'd do.'

'We'll try to see that nothing does happen, Mr. Elman.' I started for the door, half-turned and added: 'Lock the store and don't open it to anyone except the police . . . they'll be coming back here any time now.'

He sagged against the counter, splaying a veined hand hard down on it. I went back on to the little street. An automobile cruised in at the other end, but it wasn't a prowl car. I turned the corner and hurried through the crowds. It took me ten minutes to find La Jaquita Crescent and several more minutes to find the right apartment. It was on the ground floor of the seventeen hundred block, a modern block with a white trim and a brick-red roof. I leaned on the bell-push. Chimes sounded, then footsteps and the door opened and a girl with long coppery hair stood there. She was wearing a white linen dress with a polka-dot kerchief loosely knotted round her throat. She was in her middle twenties, about five feet five inches tall, and her eyes, which were a clear blue with amber flecks, regarded me levelly from the flawless oval of her face.

I took my hat off and said: 'I'm trying to locate Miss Annette Falaise and . . . ' That was as far as I got. She had stepped back and was closing the door. I wedged one of my big feet in it and went on: 'It's all right, Miss Arden — I'm a friend.'

She stared down at my foot, then up at me. 'Annette said someone might possibly come and that I was . . . '

'I'm not Dino Carelli, if that's what you're thinking, Miss Arden.'

She looked steadily at me for a long moment and slowly opened the door. 'No,' she said, 'you don't look as if you could be. Who are you?'

'Dale Shand. I had a conversation with Miss Falaise in a bar. I covered up for her when Carelli came in. She didn't want to see him.'

'Oh . . . ' She stepped back and smiled. 'Annette mentioned you. She said you were kind to her. Please come in.'

She showed me across a square hallway and into a wide lounge dotted with Swedish-styled furniture and a large Navajo rug on the woodblock floor.

'If you were kind to Annette that's good enough for me, Mr. Shand,' she said quietly. 'What can I do for you?'

I told her everything. Her eyes didn't jump uneasily like Luke Elman's. 'Annette's said nothing about a shooting, or anything like that,' she said.

'She wouldn't, Miss Arden, because she didn't witness the shooting. She had already left. But these men believe she can lead them to Carelli. They'll come after her. So if you know where she's gone, or have any idea where she's gone, will you tell me?'

She jerked a cigarette from a walnut casket and lit it, pacing the wide room with a hand cupped under her elbow.

'If you don't trust me I can take you to Police Headquarters, Miss Arden,' I said.

She smiled for the first time. A long, friendly smile. 'I'm sorry, it's not that, Mr. Shand. I was thinking about what you've just said. Of course, I'll tell you. She's driving to Mexico.'

'Driving?'

'She has a car, why shouldn't she drive?'

I hung a pipe from my teeth and said: 'She's had a lot to drink, she's been drinking all day.'

For an instant her eyes clouded. 'Yes, I know. But she was sober when she left here. I suppose the shock of seeing Dino Carelli straightened her up.'

'Mexico,' I said. 'Why the hell Mexico?'

'I think she had the idea that Dino

wouldn't be likely to show up down there.'

'It's not Dino she has to worry about, Miss Arden. How long has she been gone?'

'Two hours, about. Perhaps a little less. Why, what are you going to do?'

'I'm going after her.'

She laughed briefly. 'I thought the police want you to remain here until after the coroner's inquiry.'

'So they said, but circumstances alter cases. I'll leave them a note at my hotel. I'll be coming back, anyway.'

'Have you got your car with you?'

'No, I'll have to hire one.'

'You really believe Annette is in danger, don't you?'

'I know it. These are desperate men. They'll stop at nothing. They know who she is, they saw her go into that bar. They likely know a great deal about her.'

She stubbed out her half-smoked cigarette in a glass tray, turning the butt round and round in the grey ash as if she were thinking of something. Finally, she looked directly at me and said: 'I have a car, it's faster than Annette's. I'll drive you to Mexico. I know where she's making for — a town just across the border called Tijuana.'

'I'm a total stranger to you, Miss Arden,' I said.

'Yes, so you are.' Her candid eyes flickered. 'On the other hand, you don't look as if you'd drop a hand on a lady's thigh without permission.'

I stared. 'You have an outspoken way of putting things, Miss Arden. As to your driving me, it's nice of you to suggest it, but . . . '

'You say these men are desperate, Mr. Shand, and well-informed. Doesn't it occur to you that they could trace *me*?' She didn't wait for me to answer, but went on: 'If that's even remotely possible, I'd be safer with you.'

I dropped my pipe in my pocket and said: 'All right, I'll take your offer up.'

She smiled again. 'The car's in a garage behind the apartment. We'd better go right away, or as soon as I can throw some overnight things in a case.'

That occupied no more than minutes.

'We'll need passports,' she said. 'I've got one. How about you?'

'I brought it with me in case I decided to make a side trip to Mexico. Actually, I was going back to New York on the morning flight. I can pick the passport up at my hotel.'

'All right.' We went down to her car. It was a Studebaker, a GT model. She turned it off the concrete apron and drove expertly through the traffic. There was a vacant parking slot in front of the hotel and she slid into it. I went up to my room, peeled my jacket off and strapped a gun harness on. I took out the automatic, cleaned and oiled the mechanism, fitted a new clip of shells and thrust it in the holster.

I put my jacket back on, stuffed a shirt and pyjamas into a briefcase and was re-crossing the room when I heard the small sound of someone trying the door. I hadn't heard any footsteps. The handle turned and I flattened myself against the side of the door.

It opened inwards, almost touching me. A gun with a long silencer screwed on the barrel poked into the room.

5

The man who was holding the gun was the pale-faced boy who drove the car out to Beverly Hills. He stood just inside the room, his head craned slightly forward. I brought my right hand down in a hard chop on his shoulder. He made a small, breathy gasp and slumped to the floor.

He wasn't out, though. He rolled sideways, came half-upright, steadying himself enough to trigger the gun. But I had my own out and shot first. The slug tore into his right forearm. He yelled and toppled backwards, his weapon thudding across the carpet. I went after him, then wheeled suddenly.

Footsteps had sounded on the corridor. Then a voice. A remembered voice, the voice of the man called Frank. They had traced my hotel and I ought to have known they would do it. There could be several of them, but they had sent the pale boy on ahead. I jumped across the floor to the fire stairs. I was half-way down and out of sight round the first of two bends before they could do anything.

A minute later I was back in Julie Arden's car. She let the clutch in and moved out into the traffic stream. We were going downtown before she spoke. 'You didn't come out through the main entrance, Mr. Shand,' she said.

'I used the fire stairs.'

'You look a mite ruffled.'

'I feel like that. I had an unexpected visitor. I shot him.'

Her slim hands, lightly freckled at the knuckles, tightened imperceptibly on the wheel.

'I didn't kill him,' I said. 'He was one of the characters who kidnapped me. I guess they found the hotel I was registered at and came for me.'

'But why?'

'To stop me talking. They were going to kill me before I left that house in Beverly Hills. I guess they haven't given up the intention.'

'But you don't even *know* these dreadful men, do you?' she said.

'No. I never saw them before.'

'What on earth is it all about?'

'I don't know that, either, Julie.'

'So we're on first name terms, are we?' she said without turning.

'Well, we seem likely to spend a lot of time in somewhat close proximity.'

'Yes,' she said. 'Dale . . . it's an unusual name.'

'A little, perhaps. My old man had a friend named Warren Dale, that's how I got it.'

'I'd say you are a somewhat unusual man anyway.'

'I don't think of myself that way. A lot of the time I do pretty dull work.'

'You surprise me, I thought private eyes were always having high adventures.'

'Not always. Sometimes.'

'Like now, for instance?'

'Yeah, if I knew just what kind of adventure this was.'

She made a small sidelong glance toward me. 'You don't do horrid snooping work, do you?' she asked.

'Like peeping through keyholes to get divorce evidence, you mean? No, I don't take that sort of case.' I grinned. 'If things get tough sometime I might have to.'

'I don't believe you would, even if you struck a really bad patch,' she said evenly. 'You aren't the kind.'

'Why, do you know detectives who are?'

'No, but I've met you. I'd say you're a rather sensitive man.'

'Thanks,' I said dryly.

'Well, aren't you?'

'I've been known to get involved in situations where sensitivity didn't help. Just now, for instance.'

'That was different, it was forced on you. Besides, it wasn't what I meant. What made you become a private investigator?'

'I used to be a newspaperman. Then I became an assistant investigator attached to the District Attorney's office in New York. But I'm not a good team man and I test rather high on calculated insubordination. I got out of line once too often and started out on my own.'

'Do you like it, Dale?'

'Some of it, not all of it and not all the

time. But I'm free — or have the illusion of freedom. At least, I don't have to catch the boss's eye or take orders.'

'Not even from the clients?' she asked mockingly.

'No. If they hire me it's on the basis that I play the cards the way they fall, without interference.' I shifted slightly in my seat and added: 'I'm not saying I mean to remain a PI the rest of my life. It's a somewhat lonely occupation.'

'You mean you might go back to newspapers perhaps?'

'I don't think so. I've had some limited success with writing and I might try it full-time — creative writing I mean, not journalism.'

'That's even more lonely than being a sleuth, isn't it?'

'I guess it is, but it's safer. How about you?'

'I'm a fashion model, but that's merely to earn enough to live on. I want to paint. Well, I *do* paint. I've even had things on exhibition, but I couldn't live on painting, not yet.' She drove on for several minutes before speaking again. Then she said:

'What are we going to do when we get to Tijuana?'

'Find Annette Falaise.'

'But how? She might be anywhere.'

'We'll tour the hotels one by one until we find her. Unless she's gone to friends down there.'

'I never heard Annette mention any, so she probably has gone to a hotel.'

'We'll find out, Julie.' We were moving slowly on Olvera Street in the heart of downtown Los Angeles. A narrow street almost within the shadow of City Hall but looking as if it had been lifted bodily out of Old Mexico . . . stalls ranged under drooping trees, the aromatic savour from small cafés and the insistent throb of Latin-American music from unseen guitars. Then we were out on the broad downward sweep of the main route south with Catalina Island twenty-five miles out on the placid bosom of the Pacific. It was too dark to see the ocean, but the ceaseless murmur of the long rollers breaking on the shoreline drifted in on the warm night air.

Time passed. I lit two cigarettes and

handed one to her. 'All we know is that Annette's ex-husband beat a gunman to the draw and that the gunman was a hired killer in a mob rich enough to take over a big house in Beverly Hills,' I mused.

'It doesn't tell us much, Dale.'

'No — and maybe it doesn't matter. All I'm really worried about is getting to Annette before they do.'

'You like her, don't you?' Julie said.

'Yes. I dare say it's mixed-up with memories of her as she once was — not so long ago.' A thought came to me and I said slowly: 'It seems an unusual friendship — for you, I mean.'

'I like her, too. There's a real person under all the drinking and heartbreak. I sensed that. I tried to help her . . . '

'I'm sure you did, Julie. Perhaps it's too late, though.'

'It's never too late.'

I shrugged. 'Marrying Carelli was the worst thing she ever did, I imagine. She quit when she was on top and broke a contract to do it. The law finally caught up with Carelli and after that she was on the skids. I guess she couldn't find the inner strength to beat that.'

'I suppose not.' She fell silent and then said: 'Annette doesn't even know where her husband is. How can she possibly help these men?'

'She can't, but the point is they believe she can. If they catch up with her they . . . ' I deliberately let the sentence go unfinished.

But she wouldn't leave it that way. 'You mean they . . . they'll try to force something out of her?'

'Yeah.'

'It's horrible . . . '

'That's why we have to get to her first, Julie.'

She sent the needle climbing again, put out a hand and snapped on the radio. The hearty voice of an announcer plugging yet another breakfast cereal guaranteed to turn a timorous clerk into a superman filled the interior of the car. The commercial faded and a different voice took over, reading a police message. I was barcly listening until I heard my own name.

Los Angeles City Police are anxious to trace Dale Shand, a private detective visiting here from New York. Shand, aged thirty-eight to forty, height approximately six feet, dark hair and grey or hazel eyes, vanished from his hotel early this evening on the eve of his required appearance at a coroner's inquiry. Almost immediately after he disappeared the body of an unidentified man was found in his hotel room. The man had been shot to death . . . will anyone who believes he has seen Shand please contact . . .

I sensed that Julie Arden was looking at me, but for a long moment I sat without movement, like a stone man.

Then I heard her saying, quietly: 'You didn't kill him, Dale.' It wasn't a question.

'No,' I answered thickly. 'But he failed . . . and I guess the mob doesn't like failures, so they gave it to him.'

'You better go back, hadn't you?' she said.

'You mean I must go back and clear myself. How? Who's going to believe me? A man dead in my room, my own gun fired and me to all intents and purposes taking it on the lam . . . who is going to believe me?'

'But, Dale — you can't go on running for ever.'

'No, I know that. But I have to find Annette before I go back. I can call Captain Logan from Mexico and explain; I didn't have time to write a note.'

'Dale, please — you *must* protect yourself. I can go on alone.'

'Look, if I go back now I'll be held in custody. Maybe they'll believe me, maybe not. I don't know. But all the circumstances are against me and I have no witnesses to prove a single thing I say.'

'That house they took you to — Captain Logan will find it.'

'Could be, but I'm starting to have thoughts about that, too, Julie.'

'What do you mean?'

'It's my guess the gang will have quit the place. It figures. They wouldn't risk staying on once I had made my escape.

All right, all right . . . I know I'll have to go back and face the music in the end, but not right now. If the mob find Annette they'll torture her. The man who spoke through an amplifier made it pretty clear how they deal with reluctant victims. No, I'm going on. I'll call Logan, as I said. If we can bring Annette back with us that might help.'

'You're placing yourself on the wrong side of the law, Dale — you know that.'

'Yes, I know it. But look at it this way: I'm already on the wrong side. If I go back now I won't have even a remote chance of proving or disproving anything. They could throw the book at me and I'd have no defence.' The words sounded like something out of a thriller script. Maybe, unconsciously, they were. Words you read in a book or hear on television and marvel that a man could put himself so much in the wrong . . . until the man happens to be you.

Somehow I had to get evidence. Perhaps Annette Falaise could supply a little. She would owe me something for saving her — if we found her. I felt my jaw muscles tighten. I *had* to find her now.

Then Julie Arden was speaking again. 'You've made your mind up, haven't you?' she said. 'All right — but I'm in it with you.'

'No,' I snarled. 'You don't have to share my troubles.'

She made another of her small laughs. 'I don't have to, but I'm going to,' she said. 'And don't try to stop me because it won't be any use. Anyway, the police don't know you're with me. Nobody'll be looking for this particular make of car and we're well on the way south now.' She glanced at the gauge on the instrument panel and said: 'We're running out of petrol, the marker's almost at zero.'

Three miles down the road I said: 'We're in luck — there's a filling station coming up in your headlights.'

She cut speed, going down through the gears and drifted on to a dirt forecourt. Two stripped-down cars were on it, all open chassis and garish paintwork and twin klaxons. One of them looked like a souped-up vintage Duesenberg from way back.

Hot rods. Four boys in black leather jackets and pale blue levis lounged against them. On the backs of their jackets the crimson word *Tigers* was let into big yellow orbs. They stood sideways. Cigarettes hung laxly from their mouths. They didn't speak or move. They just stood there watching us.

The tallest of the bunch grinned and closed one eye at his companions.

6

The blue-overalled attendant piped ten gallons aboard and I paid him. Julie got out of the Studebaker to stretch her legs. The boy who had grinned took a raddled cigarette from his mouth, dropped it to the dirt ground and mashed it under the heel of his pointed shoe.

'Hi, baby,' he said.

She was half-turned from him and seemed to be unaware that he had spoken to her. He moved out, planting himself in front of her.

'Want to change cars, baby?' He asked the question in a soft purr.

'I beg your pardon,' she said.

'This guy you're with, he's too old for a cute little baby like you,' the boy went on. He gestured towards the Duesenberg. 'How's about ridin' with me? I'd show you a swell time and . . . '

She looked at him and through him. The grin faded.

'The lady is otherwise engaged,' I said.

'I'm not talking to you, dad.' He said it without even looking at me.

The attendant, a short freckled fellow, muttered uneasily: 'I don't want no more trouble, Joe . . . '

'You've had trouble before, haven't you?' I said. 'Hot-rodders like these hanging around gas stations waiting for the chance to gang-up on someone, especially if there's a girl.'

'Drop dead, dad,' the boy called Joe said. He hadn't taken his eyes off Julie. 'I just made you a proposition, baby,' he went on.

Julie said in a level tone: 'Good night . . . .' She started back for the car. The other three boys laughed. The one who had done all the talking moved forward. His face was full of blood. He was the leader of the wolf pack, he had his reputation to consider. He moved like a dancer, fast and lithe. He spun her round, holding her hard against him.

He began to bend her back, laughing. 'I got a hot way with cool chicks, baby . . . '

I felt my hand crunch into his collar. I

yanked him off her and hit him with everything I had. His feet left the dirt as he flailed backwards into the other three.

He screeched, froth bubbling on his sensual mouth. His hand jumped inside his jacket. I closed in before he could get the knife out and flick the blade open. I hit him just below the left ear. The impact turned him completely round. He swayed, teetering on his feet, then slithered down. I wheeled on his friends, but they just stood there, their eyes glaring hate and uncertainty.

The scared attendant poked my change at me. I got back in the car, behind the wheel this time, and drove away while they were still picking Joe out of the dirt.

Julie said: 'Thank you . . . ' Her voice trembled. 'If I had been alone . . . ' She stopped, then added: 'Why are boys like that so horrible?'

'Hotrodders looking for what they call fun,' I grunted. 'They hang around places like that waiting for someone to have fun with.'

'I don't understand it,' she whispered.

'Too much money, too much time and

too little discipline. I dare say that sounds out-of-date, but it happens to be true. I don't mean about all kids. There's plenty of decent young fellows, but just now there's too many like that bunch.'

'I . . . suppose they could be on LSD or something?'

'I don't think they were on a psychedelic ride,' I said. 'That kind get their kicks out of sex and sadism.'

'Well, my goodness, you certainly settled the score for them,' she said.

'Perhaps.'

'Why, what do you mean?'

'There's a car coming up fast behind us,' I said.

She stared round in her seat, saw the blinding glare of headlights. I could feel her tremble again. 'You don't think . . . '

'They'll try to get back at us, Julie. They haven't finished with us yet.' I cut the speed but stayed not too close to the grass of the tree-lined verge.

One of the rods screamed past, almost grazing us. It went on up the roadway and round a bend and vanished. More lights swept up behind us. The air was shattered by the continuous thunder of an open exhaust as it came level. It was the souped-up vintage Deusenberg. The leader of the pack was driving, his white face grinning again. He flicked the big steering wheel delicately, his mouth working in delight. He was in his element now. I swung over to the right, an instinctive reflex. The manœuvre almost sent us into the trees. The boy laughed. You couldn't hear it in the din, but you could see it. Then he was streaking for the bend at nearly a hundred miles an hour.

Julie said in a shocked voice: 'Dale ... he tried to make us crash, it was deliberate.'

'I told you they're playing a game with us. They figure it's funny.'

'For heaven's sake, we could have been killed.'

'Sure. They'd think that was funny, too.' I drove on, not fast, peering through the window. Lights blazed again. The rods were roaring straight back, one behind the other. I put the car into the verge and under the trees. The white-faced boy went past first, swerving close in again, but not close enough because of the trees. Then they were both gone. I pulled back on to the road and drove fast. A bridge loomed ahead. When we reached it I stopped on the hump.

'What are you going to do, Dale?' Her fingers gripped my arm.

'They haven't finished, they'll be back in a few minutes and this time they'll take all the chances.' As I spoke I turned the car completely round, facing back the way we had come. There was a low wall on either side of the bridge, nothing on the approach; the road merged on both sides into short grass sloping straight down to a shallow river.

'I can hear them now . . . ' she gasped the words.

They were coming side by side, klaxons blaring. I snapped all the lights of the car full on so that they got the total glare. The klaxons faded in a squeal of savagely braked tyres and crashing gear shifts.

It was over in split seconds. The rods separated, swung wildly across the road and plunged down the slopes straight into the river. The shallow water was only up to bonnet level. I could see all four of them scrambling out, shrieking obscenities.

I grinned, wheeled the car round and was going through the gears when a saloon with a light band painted on half of it cruised down the road and passed us. I didn't stop. It wasn't the time for tedious explanations; it was still less the time for tangling with the Highway Patrol.

We were about midway between Encinitas and Solana Beach on the National Interstate Highway. I wound the motor up into the high seventies and held it there. The long white road was pelting towards us, trees and telegraph poles merged in a continuous rushing mass.

A dozen miles to San Diego and the road still empty. Then, suddenly, it wasn't. I looked in the mirror. Far behind us car lights appeared like distant stars, growing larger. A siren was wailing. I rammed the pedal down to the floorboards. The road swept into a long bend and round the bend was traffic. I had to slow, but so had the Patrol.

Less than a hundred yards ahead a big truck began to lumber out from an intersection. I stabbed my foot down one more time and went past the truck with a margin of inches. I looked back. The truck was right across the road and the Highway Patrol driver was standing on everything. I could see my knuckles shining like white marbles through the tight skin of my hands on the steering wheel. But we had made it. Seven minutes later we were cruising through the city past the Civic Centre. I made a turn, skirting the Mission San Diego de Alcala and on past La Jolla and the Mount Palomar Observatory.

Julie said: 'Are we safe now?'

'Not yet. The Highway Patrol will use their radio. But unless they have the registration number of your car, which is unlikely, we'll probably get clear.'

We went through Chula Vista. Nobody even saw us. The small town was deserted at this hour. Then I gunned the motor fast down the last few miles to the frontier. Nothing happened again. We crossed the line and were in Tijuana.

A uniformed Mexican stepped out from the border post and looked casually at our passports. He also looked, not so casually, at Julie Arden. Below his slim black moustache small white teeth flashed in a smile.

'*Qué noche más agradable hace*,' he said.

Julie stared uncomprehendingly. I said: 'He is saying it is a nice evening.'

The Mexican beamed. 'You are *americano*, but you speak the Spanish, yes?'

I nodded and said: '*Cuál es el mejor hotel en esta ciudad?*'

He sighed grandiloquently. 'Your accent, *señor*, is not so good, no. Perhaps it is better you stick to the *inglés*, eh? You wish to know the best hotel in Tijuana? I tell you. It is, beyond all question, the Hotel San Luiz.' He got another beam out and hung it on his amiable face. 'My brother he is the manager, so I recommend you to him with the full confidence.'

'Thank you,' said Julie prettily.

'*Encantada, señorita.*' He bowed low, straightened-up, poked the passports back through the window and said, in English: 'The hotel is two, mebbe three minutes in your auto. You cannot mistake it, but I tell you the exact route, eh?'

'*Es usted muy amable,*' I said.

He laughed. '*Muchísimas gracias, señor* — but I still advise you to stick to the *inglés.*'

'You're probably right, *el capitano,*' I said. He was a lieutenant, but I didn't think he would resent the courtesy promotion. 'Actually, we wish to join a friend — the Senorita Annette Falaise. Perhaps you . . . ' I stopped, because the answer was already in his friendly eyes.

'*Si señor,* she arrive most recently, one hour or so ago.' He paused and then said: 'She seem a little distrait, not so well perhaps.'

'She *has* been unwell.'

'*Es muy de lamentar,*' he said sadly. Then he brightened and added: 'She is also at the Hotel San Luiz. I send her there, but naturally.'

'Assuredly, captain.'

'The wine my brother keep is most

excellent,' he rejoined. 'I specially mention this to the Señorita Falaise. She will like it.'

I thought it more than probable, but I didn't tell him.

The hotel was just off the main street midway along a winding avenue clamorous with cafés and Mexican music. I signed the register, then Julie signed. The desk clerk took two keys down from a board on the wall and was holding them out when a fine, slim Mexican of about fifty came across the foyer. He wore a fine, slim suit of midnight blue mohair, a royal blue tie with a vertical gold stripe down the centre and a lot of finely brushed silver hair above a brown, smiling face.

'Señor Fejou, the manager,' intoned the clerk deferentially.

I said: 'We were recommended here by your brother, at the frontier post.'

'*Si*, Pedro is most thoughtful. I shall endeavour to justify the commendation he has without doubt made to you.'

'I am certain of it, Mr. Fejou. By the way, I believe the Señorita Falaise, who is a friend of ours, is also staying at your admirable hotel.'

'She is registered, *si*, but has gone out and not yet has she returned.' His warm brown eyes flickered to the wall clock. 'It is now twenty minutes after twelve, but the night is yet young, eh? No doubt the *señorita* will return later.'

I was hungry, but it was more important to find Annette Falaise. We went out into the town, from one café to another. If she was out drinking she wasn't doing it in any place we visited. We went back to the hotel. The desk clerk was nodding on his stool. He awoke blinkingly: 'You wish to contact the Señorita Falaise, sir . . . alas, she has gone and is not returning.'

'Gone . . . where has she gone?' I said harshly.

'She telephone from Ensenada to say she was most regrettable but circumstances arise which prevent her from returning.'

'What circumstances — or didn't she say?'

The clerk shook his head.

'Do you know the address she was telephoning from?'

'She did not mention that, *señor*.'

'We'd better go, Julie,' I said. 'It's a straight drive on the coast road.' I turned to the desk clerk and said: 'I'm sorry, but we'll have to check out. Permit me to pay for the rooms.' I laid money in front of him and glanced in the oval mirror behind the counter. It showed me a face stiff with fatigue, or with something that made it stiff. Shand looking his age.

I went up to the room I wasn't going to occupy. I picked up the briefcase and went down the stairs to meet Julie. A man was standing in the entrance with his back to me. I couldn't see his face, but I didn't need to see it. I knew now why Annette Falaise had left in a hurry.

He was Dino Carelli.

7

Julie Arden came down the curving stairway. I put out a hand and held her arm, steering her sideways through an arched opening into the *salon*.

'My goodness, you look as if you'd seen a ghost,' she joked.

'No ghost, Julie. I've just seen Dino Carelli.'

'What!'

'He's in the hotel, that was him with his back to us.'

Her eyes widened. 'You mean he's come here to find Annette?'

'I shouldn't think he has. It's more likely that he lammed-off into Mexico after the killing. If he was driving it'd be over the same route we took, so he would be bound to enter via Tijuana. I imagine he was here first and that Annette spotted him and took fright. It would . . . '

I broke off, listening. Carelli was saying something to the desk clerk in laboured

Spanish, but I caught the words all right — '*Me permite que haga una llamada desde su teléfono?*'

The clerk told him where the telephone booth was. I had seen it before, it was close to the archway. I could hear Carelli walking towards it. I inched myself round to see him. He was inside the booth with his back still toward me. The door of the booth wasn't fully closed. He was speaking into the mouthpiece, but I missed what he was saying. So I moved a little more out.

There was a pause. He filled it in by striking a match on the glass of the booth and lighting a panatella. Then his call went through and he started speaking again.

'Carelli here . . . yeah, Dino Carelli, the one your trouble boys tried to kill . . . ' He made a low, rasping sound that wasn't quite a laugh. 'They must've been tailing me. They sent Fatso in with a gun. He ain't fast enough . . . well, he won't be able to try again. I put the chill on him . . . ' He paused, blew a thin stream of cigar smoke at the mouth-piece until it billowed out in small blue clouds. Then he snarled: 'Shut up! I'm doing the talking this time. I'm in Mexico for a little whiles until the johns turn the heat off. Then I'm coming back and I'm taking over . . . where I left off. Just tell Johnny he better be watching out is all . . . '

He hung up with a sharp click and I ducked back. There was a door at the other end of the *salon*. We went through it, found our way to the forecourt and got back in the Studebaker.

We were out on the coast road going south when Julie said: 'What was all that?'

'Carelli on the telephone.' I repeated the substance of what he had said. 'He was calling someone connected with the fellows who kidnapped me. I'd say that when he was sent to the pen he was usurped by somebody and he was warning them that he means to assume control again. Unfortunately, I don't know who he was calling.'

'Do you suppose he knows Annette has been here, Dale?'

'I doubt it. He wouldn't expect to see her in this place.'

'Suppose the clerk mentions her?'

'Why should he? He doesn't know there's any connection between them. The only chance of Carelli knowing is if he happens to read the hotel register. She's registered under her own name. Anyway, he can't have done it yet.'

'And if he does?'

'I don't know. He might want to find her — on the other hand, he might not. After all, they've been washed-up so far as their marriage goes for years.'

A threequarter moon sailed out from drifting cloud. Pale lunar radiance bathed the landscape and the night air was heavy with the pungent scents of Mexico. We went through Rosarito Beach and El Descanso, almost hugging the Pacific shoreline. The road was paved but uneven in places; if you wanted a modern freeway with a manic torrent of traffic you would have to go to Mexico City, with its five million citizens, its slender glass-walled apartment blocks rearing skywards from brownish land strewn with tin and clap-board shanties, its high-walled villas with their private swimming pools and, just outside them, the peasants taking water from trucks and carrying it home in battered cans strapped to the aching backs of crushed donkeys.

For the rest, if you are coming in from the United States you soon find that Mexico means the end of the six-lane interstate turnpikes and the beginning of a semi-arid waste-land with slick technological advancement jostling age-long poverty and squalidly picturesque Indian mud huts. You are glad you filled the tank of your car before you left the U.S., because it will pink like crazy on Mexican gasolene. We had five gallons left, which wasn't likely to be enough.

It was long after one in the morning when we went through the last village before Ensenada. Even at this hour donkeys still nibbled at the short tufts of grass thrusting up through the cobbles of a street which cleaved between wood fences and crumbling houses. A few more miles and we were there. Ensenada is a resort almost at the northern tip of the Sierra San Pedro Martir. A good spot to idle in with a pretty girl if you aren't troubled by murders, kidnapping and the apparently insoluble reasons why.

We went into the first hotel we saw. The foyer was small and green-tiled and twin palms grew one on either side of the desk. A wood screen carried the sign *El Dueno*, but the proprietress wasn't on duty. Nor was the clerk. Only a yawning night porter whose coppery face and high cheek-bones announced the mingling of Indian blood in his veins. About ten per cent of Mexicans speak no Spanish, using upwards of fifty Indian dialects instead, but since he was a hotel employee the chances were that he wasn't one of them.

I tried, speaking slowly: '*Vive aqui el Señorita Falaise?*' I had to do it twice more before he understood. Then he merely shook his head.

I described her to him and this time he nodded eagerly. Then he began speaking — too fast for me to grasp what he was saying first and second times. But in the end I got it.

'She stopped-off here and telephoned through to the hotel in Tijuana — then she drove right on,' I said.

'What do we do now?' asked Julie simply.

I grunted. 'I'm tired and you're tired. I'm calling it a day. She took the road south to San Vicente. Maybe she'll feel safe there. We'll find her tomorrow. Right now all I want to find is some sleep.'

'I'm terribly tired,' she said with a smile.

I asked the porter if they had rooms. They had plenty. He thumbed a bell, waited a moment, then chanted: '*La doncella . . . La doncella . . .* '

A stout chambermaid came from the back of the hotel with a swish of shining black skirts and showed us where the rooms were and went away.

Julie said: 'It . . . it's been quite a day, hasn't it?'

'Yeah. We'll make an early start in the morning.' Suddenly, it came to me that even after hours sitting close together in an automobile we knew little about each other. There had been small interludes of partial self-revelation, but too many incidents involving action and flight. We knew little of each other's backgrounds, habits, preferences; didn't even know what kind of food we liked. Yet in some indefinable way, I felt that I knew her to the point at which words almost ceased to matter.

I looked down at the pale oval of her face, the wide candid eyes, the soft curve of her figure under the linen dress. She looked back calmly. If there was an expression in her eyes I didn't know what it was.

'I think I'm going to like you — a lot,' she said. She brushed her mouth very quickly against mine and was gone.

The door closed behind her. I stood there looking at it. I lifted knuckles to tap on the panelling. I wasn't aching with fatigue. I didn't any longer want sleep, unless it was lying next to her with my arms holding her. If I knocked she would open the door and I could walk in. She couldn't stop me and maybe I could have her, or take her.

I dropped my hand from the door and went into my room. The door was on the latch. I supposed the chamber-maid had left it unlocked. I pushed on in and a voice spoke out of the darkness.

'The light switch is on your left, *señor*. Press it down, but do not otherwise move.' A deep chuckle welled out. 'That is, unless you desire me to fire the gun I am holding. It is looking directly at you . . .'

8

I got the lights on and saw him. He was sitting on the edge of the bed with his feet crossed on the floor, but it didn't make him look negligent. He was a heavy man but not more than two hundred and sixty pounds. His face, which was the colour of a pickled walnut, looked as if it had been scarred and battered in a hundred fights. He wore a heavy pale blue shirt with a stitched collar, heavy corded riding pants thrust into hand-tooled boots, and a heavily-ringed hand wrapped itself around a heavy .45 Colt automatic as if it were a toy pistol. Any way you looked at him he was heavy.

'*Está usted en su casa*,' he said. The voice matched the rest of him; it was as heavy as a waterlogged boat.

I stayed where I was and he went on, in English: 'I invited you to make yourself at home, but if you prefer to do it standing up it is okay by me *señor*. You will doubtless desire me to explain the purpose of this visit.'

'Some such thought had occurred to me,' I said.

He grinned without showing any teeth. 'I am Gonzales. I am the agent here of The Organization.' He eyed me expectantly, as if the statement called for some reaction. 'You have nothing to say, Mr. Shand? That is surprising.'

'I haven't the slightest idea what you are talking about, Mr. Gonzales.'

He studied me frowningly. 'You have the appearance of one who speaks the truth as he knows it, yet it is strange that you do not know of The Organization.'

'How do you know my name and how the hell did you get in here?' I asked.

He shrugged without changing the position of his gun. 'There is, but naturally, a rear entrance to the hotel. I entered that way in order to be as unobtrusive as possible. Your name, *señor*, was furnished by a confidant.'

'The night porter left us for a few moments,' I remembered. 'I suppose he telephoned you.'

'Si. All agents have been asked by The Organization to look out for you. Just routine, you onnerstan'. They do not know in which direction you have gone when you leave Los Angeles so abruptly. Thus all agents are asked to keep the eye open. It is my good luck that you come to Ensenada.'

'What's so lucky about it, Mr. Gonzales?'

His bushy eyebrows lifted. 'The Organization will be most grateful to me for apprehending you, Mr. Shand.'

'You're not police, Mr. Gonzales. I'd say you don't have much standing with them in Ensenada.'

'They view me with the suspicion, si. That is why I enter the hotel so quietly.' He chuckled again, a deep-toned chuckle oozing up through layers of fat. 'The coppers they would much like to — how you say? — make the pinch, but they have nothing on me. And soon perhaps it is Gonzales who will tell them some few things.'

'I'm beginning to get the idea,' I said. 'The Organization plan to infiltrate here, you mean?'

'Already the preliminary steps are taken, Señor Shand. The day will arrive when we control everything in Ensenada, also elsewhere — all over the United States.'

'But the day is not yet, so you have to sneak up the back stairs like the cheap hoodlum you are.'

His black eyes glittered. Then he laughed. 'You wish to provoke me into making some unguarded move, eh? I am not so simple, Mr. Shand. But do not try me too far. The Organization wish me to deliver you to them alive . . . but my instructions do not preclude killing you, should that become necessary.'

'So you're taking me somewhere?'

'But of course. It is the purpose of my unconventional visit. I have the car waiting behind the hotel. I place the manacles on your wrists and drive you across the border to San Diego, where some representatives of The Organization will be waiting. The *señorita* who has come here with you I care nothing about. I have no orders about her.'

'How about Annette Falaise?'

His face darkened. 'She is here and she is gone before I can act. Is most regrettable. But I have taken care of that, for always I am the efficient one.'

'Not efficient enough to catch her on the run,' I sneered.

'You think not? That is because you are the fool. I know where she has gone, it is to San Vicente. So I telephone our agent there. Felipe Joacim will be waiting for her and . . . ' He broke off, grinning. 'Perhaps you are not quite such a fool. You tricked me into saying that. So now you know who our agent is in San Vicente. But no good will the knowledge do you.' He stood up abruptly. The automatic was rock-steady in his right hand. With the other he slipped handcuffs out of a pocket. 'I must now ask you to extend both the wrists, Señor Shand . . . '

I still had my back to the wall. I inched my shoulder upwards until it touched the light switch. I held both hands out. Then, as he closed in, I pushed the switch off. In the same instant I dived for his legs. The automatic slammed out of his grip as I took him in a football tackle. He hit the floor like a dropped sandbag. I drove a knee upwards and he screamed. One of his enormous hands clawed at my face, forcing it back. I sunk a short punch into his belly. The hand went away. I rolled clear, jumped up and lunged across the dark room.

He came after me, a mass of lumbering sound. But I had found the switch again. When I got the lights back on I had my own gun out with the muzzle rammed into his chest. He looked down at it, then up. His heavy battered face was a ravaged mask of naked terror.

I said tightly: 'The Organization killed a man who failed to take me, Mr. Gonzales. I'm afraid you'll have to abandon all ideas about playing Mr. Shot in Ensenada . . . assuming you go on living.'

He swayed slightly on the end of the gun. 'What are you going to do, *señor*?' he whispered.

'I'm taking you for a ride, Mr. Gonzales. Not the kind you were going to take me on. Just a ride into the country.' I reached for the fallen handcuffs. 'We're going to walk out of this hotel like nothing has happened. Only don't try anything because I'll be two paces behind you with the gun in my pocket. All right, start walking.'

We went out of the room. Julie's door was next to mine. I knocked on it after all. She came out in pyjamas. I said: 'I haven't time to explain. Just get clothes on and pack your case. We're leaving.'

Her wide eyes flickered to Gonzales. But she didn't ask questions. Inside three minutes she was ready. We went down the back stairs. Nobody saw us. I put the handcuffs on Gonzales and pushed him down on the rear seats of the car and drove south. Ten miles beyond Maneadero I hauled him out, marched him to the edge of a cliff overlooking the ocean.

He moaned: 'Don't kill me . . . Mother of God, don't kill me. I am not ready to die.'

I put the gun on him and thrust him down the long rutted slope to a strip of beach white in the moonlight.

'Turn round,' I said.

He came round slowly. 'I only obey the instructions, señor,' he said. 'I mean you no harm personally — *Le ruego me perdone.*'

'It's not my forgiveness you want, it's your life, Gonzales. You can have it on one condition.'

He stared dumbly at his shackled hands. 'The Organization kill me if I betray them,' he whispered.

I grinned at him. 'And Shand kills you if you don't — take your choice, Mr. Gonzales.'

'What is it you wish me to tell you?' His voice had sunk to a faint rustle, like dead leaves drifting on concrete.

'The name of the man who runs The Organization will do.'

He shook. 'Please, I do not know . . . you must believe me.' He fought to regain some shreds of human dignity and said: 'If you decide to kill me I still cannot tell you what I do not know, *señor.*'

I didn't think he was lying. Few men lie when they believe their lives are the price of their falsehoods. 'All right,' I said.

'Let's try it another way. Who gives you the orders?'

He ran his tongue across dry lips and said: 'Señor Malone.'

'A fine old Irish name,' I grunted.

'*Perdón*'

'What's his first name?'

'Frank. Señor Frank Malone.'

I described the smooth, beautifully-tailored man who had sat in the kidnap car, a thousand years ago it seemed. Gonzales nodded his vast head.

'What orders does Malone give you, apart from the one about me in case I showed up in Mexico?'

'I am appointed to represent The Organization in Ensenada and to establish it here . . . '

'Like recruiting a bunch of hoodlums, for instance?'

'I enlist the co-operation of trusted friends, *si*. We are to be ready when the moment comes.'

'Ready for what — to organize protection, take over gambling, vice, entertainment?'

He shrugged, not speaking.

'What about other places in Mexico?'

'The Organization is still appointing agents, *señor*. In Mexico City and elsewhere.'

'And you don't know who the real boss is?'

'*Señor*, I have told you. I know nothing of this man, except . . . ' He wetted his dry lips again and said: 'Except that I think he is from New York.'

'What do you mean, you think he is?'

'It is just a thought I have, *señor*. I think Frank Malone is come from there. I do not know this for certain, I think it.'

'You must have a reason.'

'No, *señor*. Only that I hear him mention New York once. Perhaps it does not mean anything.'

I stared past him. Mist was rising from the long swell of the Pacific. The rollers almost lapped our feet, but they wouldn't come any closer because the tide was starting to ebb. I put the gun back in its clip and said: 'You've bought your freedom, Mr. Gonzales.'

'You are not going to kill me, then?'

I grinned sardonically. 'I wasn't going

to even if you hadn't talked. *Adios*, Mr. Gonzales. You'll have to hike it back to Ensenada. It'll take a long time, but you'll have your troubled thoughts for company. *Feliz viaje.*'

I climbed back up the cliff. Julie was sitting in the car smoking a cigarette.

'I've left our friend on the beach,' I said. 'That puts him out of circulation for a while.' I told her what Gonzales had said and started driving back on to the road. 'We'd better get to San Vicente . . . '

'Dale, we could be too late if this man Joacim has already been contacted.'

'We have to try, Julie.'

She stubbed the cigarette out and threw it away. 'I saw a pay telephone booth as we went through the last town — Maneadero, I think it was.'

I laughed dryly. 'You're a better detective than I am just at this moment, Julie.'

'Well, you could find this man Joacim's number and call him, pretending to be somebody from The Organization.'

'Yes,' I agreed. 'It might work, at that.'

We went back to Maneadero. The telephone booth was on the main street. But you had to feed counters in the slot, not coin money. It was after three o'clock in the morning and the whole place was sleeping, or seemed to be. Then I found a café with lights still on behind its closed doors. I knocked up the proprietor and bought a handful of tokens. There was a directory in the booth. I found Joacim's number and called it.

A furry voice answered: '*Digame! oiga!*'

'Señor Felipe Joacim? This is The Organisation.'

The voice lost its furriness. 'Sorry, Señor Joacim is out. Who is speaking?'

'Malone.' I tried to make my voice sound something like his.

But it didn't matter because the man at the other end replied: 'Señor Malone — I have not the pleasure of addressing you before.'

'Where's Joacim?'

'Señor Gonzales telephone that the Señorita Falaise, one of the persons you wish to contact, is on her way here. Felipe is dealing with this in person.'

I snarled down the line. 'Why hasn't he contacted us?'

The voice sounded bewildered. 'He said he was going to phone you before he took off.' Then the bewilderment subsided. 'Perhaps he has not yet had the time to make the call. Be assured he will do so before he leaves.'

'What do you mean, take off?'

'I am most sorry, *señor*. Permit me to explain. Felipe located the *señorita*'s hotel. He has gone there. He is driving her to the airstrip. He has the charter plane always ready, as you know. He is taking her to Winslow to await your pleasure.'

Winslow was in Arizona on the edge of the Painted Desert, about two hundred and fifty miles due west of Albuquerque.

'Why Winslow?' I said.

'Felipe think it safer not to take her to a large airport. He is phoning the agent in Phoenix as well as yourself so that arrangements can be made to meet him. You see, Señor Malone, all is organized most efficiently. There is nothing to worry about.'

'Not a thing,' I said thickly.

9

I drove fast back to Ensenada. They have an airport there. There was no scheduled flight to anywhere until 9 a.m., and that was more than four hours away. I turned from the Information Desk and a smiling young Mexican wearing flying clothes touched my arm.

'I have a plane available on charter, señor,' he said. 'I can be ready in twenty minutes.' He sighed. 'I regret that the cost will be considerable.'

'How considerable?'

He told me. 'We'll take it,' I said.

'Excellent, señor.' He smiled happily. 'My name is Juan. Be here in twenty minutes precisely. The bar is still open, should you desire refreshment.'

He went away and we went into the bar. I drank a large whisky which tasted good enough to be Haig and Haig.

'What about my lovely Studebaker?' wailed Julie.

'Put it on the airport parking lot. We'll come back for it some time.'

She looked at me. 'Well!' she said. But she put it on the parking lot. I drank the rest of my drink and called Central Homicide in Los Angeles. Captain Logan wasn't there. Lieutenant Hammer was.

'Shand!' His voice had a gritty edge to it, as if he were swallowing something he didn't much like. 'So you've come through at last.'

'That's right, lieutenant.'

'Where the hell are you speaking from, goddam you?'

'Ensenada.'

'Mexico . . . ' He savoured the word incredulously. Then he said: 'So you've lammed-off?'

'No. I found that Annette Falaise had gone to Tijuana. I knew that she was in personal danger. I went after her. I wanted to warn her, and also bring her back to Los Angeles.'

'Oh, yeah? Don't go simple on me, Shand.'

'I'm not making this up, lieutenant,' I said patiently.

'If she went to Tijuana what're you doing in Ensenada?'

'It's a long story.'

'I've got all night, Shand.'

'I haven't, lieutenant. I'll have to condense it. Will you listen without making noises?'

I could hear his harsh breathing, then words. 'All right, talk it up.'

I told him, all of it.

'Okay,' he snapped. 'So you beat it out of L.A. without making a required statement to chase after this broad. You don't find her. You don't find anything.'

'I was under the impression I had found something relevant.'

'Yeah — well, maybe. This outfit you call The Organization — what is it?'

'I don't know, not in a specific sense.'

'You don't know much, do you?'

'I said I don't know specifically. I have ideas, though.'

'Such as what?'

'I'd have thought the obvious thing is that The Organization is some new crime development, a variant of The Syndicate.'

Hammer breathed harshly again, but

when he answered his voice was rather less aggressive. 'You could be right, at that,' he said slowly.

'The man who was found dead in my hotel room,' I said suddenly. 'Am I to take it that the Los Angeles police think I killed him?'

He didn't make a direct answer. Instead, he said: 'The guy had been wounded before he was killed. Two different slugs. I guess you didn't use two weapons. Just the same, we want you back here — immediately, understand?'

'What about Annette Falaise?'

'I'll call the local law at Winslow and have that charter plane met. If she's on it they'll take care of her. It still sounds kind of crazy to me. You sure you're levelling with us?'

'I told you I'm not making this up. Why should I?'

'You could be covering for yourself in some way.'

'Be your age, lieutenant. What could I hope to buy with a story like that, if it was untrue?'

'Time perhaps.'

'Time for what? To make a getaway? I'm already in Mexico, didn't you hear? If I don't choose to come back you'll have a lot of tiresome paper work to do trying to have me extradited, and by that time I could be anywhere.'

Hammer said savagely: 'You better come right back, Shand.'

'I'll return, lieutenant. But the immediate concern is Miss Falaise. She's being met at Winslow by some members of this gang. I'd like to feel very sure that the local law will be there to protect her.'

'They know their job, I guess.'

'I hope so.'

'You didn't make out so well yourself trying to protect her,' sneered Hammer. 'The way you tell it, they snatched her right under your nose.'

'Not quite that, lieutenant. You'll be seeing me.' I put the phone back on its rest. Julie was beside me again.

'What was all that?' she said. 'I only caught the last part.'

'The Los Angeles City Police Department — specifically, Lieutenant Hammer of Central Homicide.'

'You mean you're going back there?'

'Yes, but not just yet.'

The smiling young Mexican flyer strolled up. 'Señor and señorita — the plane she is now ready,' he announced.

Five minutes later we were airborne. We sat side by side. Julie's head fell against my chest. I let it stay there, with her hair in my mouth and the small perfume from it filling my nostrils. I closed a hand on hers. She pressed it upwards against my palm, just the once. In another minute she was asleep.

Time passed. The pilot said we were over the border. He lit a cigarette. More time passed.

'Tucson is below us on our left señor,' he said. 'Our altitude is twelve thousand feet, air speed two hundred and twenty miles an hour. Now I have to make a small detour — I have to use the prescribed lanes for a charter flight.'

Dawn was breaking, spearing pale fingers across the vast sky. 'If you look down you will observe the tops of the mountains, señor. You can even see Fort Apache if the light is strong enough.'

'I can hardly wait,' I grunted.

Then the sun broke through, the blazing inexorable sunlight they have in the clear, rarefied air of Arizona. I saw Fort Apache for the first time.

We went beyond the White Mountains. He turned the plane slightly, going diagonally towards Winslow. Suddenly, he said: 'There is heavy cloud below us, señor. It is most unusual in this territory. I shall have to wait for instructions from Ground Control.'

Julie came awake. 'What's the matter?'

'Cloud. The pilot is getting instructions, it's all right.'

I went forward to him. He was using the radio telephone. I could hear the unemotional voice of the Controller.

'I'll have to talk you down, V for Victor Orange. Temporary cloudbank, but fairly dense. It has to be two hundred feet from ground level with forward visibility half a mile as a minimum safety condition.'

'Okay, I circle round.'

There was a pause, then the control started sending out a stream of radio beams and began the talk-down in conjunction with the instrument landing system.

The ground voice came on again: 'A ninety degrees turn now . . . okay, that's fine.'

Another pause. 'Your rate of descent is six hundred feet a minute in the glide path . . . you are above your glide path . . . increase your rate of descent until correction is made. Understood?'

'Understood.' The pilot reached for the lateral and horizontal controls, made the necessary correction and brought the plane back on the path.

He grinned jubilantly at me. 'We are coming in most nicely now, *señor*.'

Julie moved up. Her hand sought mine. The little plane went down through dense cloud which blotted out everything. But in another minute it had broken clear. The runway swept out before us like an endlessly flowing white ribbon. Then the small bump as the wheels made contact.

'You brought us in very well, Juan,' said Julie with a smile.

'*Señorita* . . . for you I do it a thousand

times,' he said. His eyes regarded her with open admiration. 'Correction — a million times!'

'I think he likes me,' murmured Julie.

'Who wouldn't?'

'Well, you haven't said anything so pretty to me, yet.'

I circled an arm round her shoulders and held her close to me. She put her face up to be kissed.

'Why, Dale,' she said, 'you're trembling.' I felt about sixteen and that was a long time ago.

We said farewell to Juan and walked across the apron to the airport buildings. The freak cloud was already dispersing and everything looked dazzling white again under the Arizona sun. We were through Customs when a siren wailed outside. I looked through the wide sweep of the window. A police car with a cowled light roared up. Three men jumped from it, one of them in civilian clothes. He led the two bluecoats in, looked at Julie and then at me. I gave him the big Shand smile. It didn't work — but, then, it hardly ever does.

He turned and said: 'Miss Annette Falaise?'

'I'm afraid not,' said Julie. 'My name happens to be Julie Arden.'

He stared and started to say something when an airport official scampered toward us, waving his arms. When he was close he gasped: 'Not this plane, Lieutenant Keller . . . '

Keller's sharp face reacted. 'Wuddia mean, not this plane?'

'You're late, lieutenant. The charter plane from San Vicente touched-down about twenty-five minutes ago.'

'Hell!' said Keller. He looked at us. 'My apologies to you both for the intrusion. We were delayed by a blow-out and a fallen tree — lightning.'

'Why, that's all right, lieutenant,' said Julie. She looked as if she were about to offer an explanation. I pinched her arm and she stopped.

Keller asked the official: 'Which way did they go when they left here and how many were there?'

The other shrugged. 'The pilot took off again for San Vicente within fifteen

107

minutes. He brought a sick lady with him. She was helped from the plane by three men. I do not know where they went, lieutenant.'

'Hell!' said Keller again. 'Well, we can't help acts of God like blow-outs and lightning, I guess. I'll have a radio call put out to all law enforcement departments in the State. What kind of car were they driving?'

The airport official spread both arms helplessly. 'I didn't see it. I supposed they were taking her to a car, but I didn't see it.'

Keller made a spitting sound without actually spitting and strode out to the police car with the bluecoats flanking him.

We went through into the lounge. A scrubwoman carrying a mop and pail came out of a door marked *Ladies*. I said: 'I suppose you didn't happen to see three men and a sick lady get into a car about a half-hour ago, or a little less?'

She answered immediately. 'Yes, I saw them. The poor lady looked real ill.'

'What kind of car was it?'

'I don't know much about cars, sir, I never had the money to own one. But it was a saloon, two-tone — dark blue and a kind of beige. I was looking on account of the poor sick lady.'

It seemed too much to expect, but I asked her just the same. 'Any idea where they were heading?'

'Why, yes. I heard the driver say they was going across the desert to Jadito Trading Post.'

I took out a ten dollar note and gave it to her. She stared at it almost disbelievingly. 'It's all right,' I said. 'You've earned it.'

There was a self-drive automobile bureau just inside the lounge near the main doors and it was open for business. I put some in their way. We washed-up and ate scrambled eggs and bacon while they got the car ready.

The sun was like a ball of fire in the sheer blue of the sky when we drove up the long paved road which skirts the Painted Desert. The air was light and dry, like a sparkling champagne, and almost as heady.

'What are we going to do if we catch-up with them, Dale?' said Julie.

'Call in the local law, I guess.'

'Suppose they don't believe us or there isn't either the time or the opportunity to call them in?'

'Now you're making difficulties . . . '

'They're more likely to be ready-made. What then?'

'I'll think of something, Julie,' I said. What I was actually thinking was that I had only once before worked alongside a girl. That was when Nancy, who operates the telephone switchboard in the mid-town apartment house where I live, practically pushed herself into a case. I was worried for her . . . and now I was worried for Julie. Somehow I would have to think of a way to keep her out of the danger line. I didn't think it would be easy.

I was driving an open convertible, a two-year-old Buick not unlike the one I own, only mine is twice the age. But the gear-shift was the same and I was at ease with it from the start.

'Are you afraid, Julie?'

'No, not really. I suppose I ought to be, but I'm not. It must be the excitement.'

I glanced off the hot paved road. To our left there was nothing now but the endless vista of sand and sparse out-crops of earth, coarse grass and tall spiky cactus trees, gaunt and ravaged in the heat. You could see ahead for miles, but there was no sign of the car we were chasing. I drove on, mile after mile. Then, suddenly, I saw it . . . not a car. A speck low down on the distant rim of the horizon, growing.

'Dale — what is it?' said Julie.

'I don't know this territory, but it looks like a dust cloud.' In a few minutes I knew exactly what it was. A swirling ball of alkali dust, enlarging and choking. Then the wind . . . harsh and gritty and driving. I stopped the car and yelled to Julie. 'It's a desert storm . . . duck right down . . . keep your hands over your face while I get the top up.'

The wind lashed into me, like a gigantic blow-torch. But I got the convertible top up, slammed the windows tight and dragged a rug off the rear seat down over us. We crouched, huddled together, half-suffocated by the heat and choking on mouthfuls of sand. The sand was everywhere . . . in our mouths, ears, nostrils, inside our clothes.

The whirl was all around us now, blotting out all light and every other sound. A dropped megaton bomb would have sounded like a muffled cough in the shrieking climactic darkness.

Then, as suddenly as it had begun, the storm swept over us and past us. The blackness was gone, the sun shone from a cloudless azure sky with a bland assurance as if nothing had ever happened to mask its warmth and geniality.

I pushed sand out of my hair. But the stuff was all over me. I got out of the car and stripped off clothes and shook them and put my trousers back on.

Julie leaned out of the car and said: 'I saw you without your clothes on.'

'Tut-tut!'

'Well, not all of you, but more than is usually considered proper.'

'You'd better take yours off and shake them out.'

'I'm going to.'

'I might look, too.'

'I'd better do it on the other side of the car then — and mind you stay right where you are.'

She got out. Her back was toward me. I could see part of her. She was pulling things off. I waited a little while. Then I started round the side of the car. She heard me coming and looked up with a small withdrawn smile. She had clothes back on, but not many. I didn't speak. I took her in my arms and kissed her mouth, her eyes, her neck. She clung to me wordlessly, her hands moving round my shoulders and down my naked back.

The sand was hot and prickly under us, but it was only later that we were conscious of it.

10

There was less sand under the car bonnet than I had expected, but I had to clean out the carburettor and air filter before the motor would start again.

The roadway was still awash with sand, but we kept on it. Ten miles slid behind us in silence, then Julie said: 'I'm very fond of you, Dale.'

'I'm fond of you.'

'Yes, I noticed that.'

'Did you know I wanted you?'

'Oh, yes. It was in your eyes when we said good night in the hotel at Ensenada.'

'I nearly knocked on your door.'

'Why didn't you?'

'I don't really know.'

'Were you shy?'

'No, it wasn't that. I don't know what it was.'

'You weren't shy just now.' She laughed. 'I never imagined myself being seduced on the edge of a desert. My goodness, I'll be tasting sand for the next week.' She pressed her hand on my thigh.

'Don't *do* that,' I said, 'or I'll wobble off the road, what there is of it to see.'

'Well, I shouldn't mind. We can stop again, if you like.'

'I'm coming up to forty,' I said.

'What's that got to do with it?'

'I need more time to recover than I did when I was coming up to twenty.'

'Why, did you have much experience at that age?'

'Not much, not like some of the kids today.'

'You make love very nicely and gently,' she said. 'I suppose you've had lots of experience since you passed twenty.'

'Not so much as you probably think, or I'd like to think.'

'You're really rather reserved, aren't you?'

'A bit, yes.'

'I mean I can tell you're determined and terribly independent and you sometimes talk in a kind of tough, worldly way, but I think you're different underneath. I think you're a very, very nice man.'

'Thanks.'

'You've never been married, have you?'

'No. I dare say I've left it too late. When a man gets to my age he's likely to be set in his ways and too selfish to make a good husband.'

She didn't answer. I drove on a short distance and said: 'How about you?'

'What about me?'

'Have you been married?'

'Yes.'

'And now you're not?'

'What makes you say that? Oh, I see. You mean there's no husband around.'

'I hope not. I don't lay other men's wives.'

'Some men think it's safer, don't they?'

'Yes, but I don't care to do it. I had a feeling you had been married, though.'

'Do you want me to tell you about it?'

'I think so. I'm interested. Anything about you interests me now.'

She looked down at her folded hands and said: 'I was seventeen and my parents didn't think Gary was good enough for me. They were right, but at seventeen you know it all. So I ran away with him. He

116

was ten years older than me. It lasted three months.'

'What went wrong?'

'He was a compulsive chaser. He couldn't keep his hands off anything in skirts, from high school girls to women old enough to be his mother.' She looked sideways at me. 'You're not like that,' she said.

'Even though I've just made love to you in the middle of the Painted Desert?'

'On the edge of it.' She smiled her wide, warm smile. 'Yes, you've had me and you've had other girls, but you're not a chaser, I can tell.'

'Now you're throwing woman's intuition at me.'

'Well, there *is* such a thing. It doesn't always work, but it works over some things. Especially over men. Not at seventeen, though. I thought Gary was the most wonderful man in the world. It wasn't very pleasant finding out what he really was.'

'You caught him out, you mean?'

'No, it wasn't like that. He was away on a business trip and the first night he called me on the phone and said he'd committed adultery.'

'Why did he tell you?'

'Remorse. And the other compulsion he had . . . the need to confess.'

'Yes, there are guys like that. And then?'

'It happened again and again. He used to come home and confess his sins to me and beg forgiveness and promise never to do it again. It was horrible. He used to break down and cry like a little boy. I was even sorry for him at first, until I found that confessing his lapses was merely a way of rationalizing them to himself and getting rid of them so that he could start all over again.'

'Not a nice thing to happen to a young girl,' I said.

'No, it was so . . . so degrading having him fornicate and then sob on my neck.' She fell silent for a long moment, then said: 'He wasn't unkind to me, you know. He was charming and considerate, especially about little things, the little things a woman likes a man to remember.'

'Yes, he probably would be, that kind of man often is.' I grinned. 'Nobody ever told me I was. But I've never lived with a woman, or not long enough to find out. What happened in the end?'

'You'll never believe it. He went off with the widow of a Texas oil millionaire. She was at least twenty years older. I divorced him and they married. They're living now in Cannes.' She laughed again. 'It might even work out — Gary needs a mother more than a wife.'

'That sounded a mite catty.'

'I didn't mean it to be. I meant it quite seriously. She's probably good for him . . . and she'll know how to handle him better than a seventeen-year-old bride did.'

'So he's stayed married?'

'Oh, yes. Eight years. He sends me a picture postcard every once in a while. I don't suppose he's been faithful to her, but I guess it's working out just the same.'

'And you've never married again yourself?'

'No. I'm not sure that I want to. What I mean to do very soon is quit modelling and become a fashion designer. I've some talent and I think a chance is coming my way soon. And, of course, I mean to paint. How far are we from Jadito?'

'Not far. We ought to be there in twenty minutes or so.'

The contours of the road were still blurred with piled and drifting sand, but I kept on. Thirty minutes later I knew the road must have forked and that we had gone down the wrong one. A sign loomed ahead, announcing: *Leupp — 17 Miles*.

It was too late to turn back. There was a map folder in the glove compartment. I got it out and said: 'We can go north from Leupp to a place called Oraibi and then back-track to Jadito — that way we might even meet them head-on.'

'Anything you like,' she said.

Leupp is on the Little Colorado River. We went through it and took the winding road up the other side of the desert. It was mid-morning and the sun wasn't yet at its peak, but it felt like burning fingers on your skin.

A lot of miles going north. Another

sign. Giant red letters on a white base: *El Reno Filling Station and Café: No more Gas for 60 Miles.* I looked at the fuel gauge. It wasn't even near zero, but it might be as well to tank up. I drove on to the forecourt. A blond kid with a face tanned the colour of old teak came up. I asked him to fill the tank, check the oil, water and battery and get rid of any remaining sand particles.

He took a drinking straw from his mouth and said: 'Sure. You folks want to eat or get some cawfee, it's ready.'

We went into the café. Just a semi-bare room in a white frame building. Coloured tables, a juke box, a long counter and behind the counter a sawn-off runt of a man with ratty brown hair and restless eyes.

'It's too hot to eat cooked food,' Julie said. 'I'll have coffee and a salad sandwich.'

I nodded. The counterman made coffee and started fixing the sandwiches.

'Come far, folks?' He asked the question without looking at us.

'A good way, yes. We hit a storm on the

edge of the desert and took the wrong route.'

'You did?' He leaned a little over the counter, reached a lighted cigarette up from a shelf underneath, dragged on it and put it back out of sight. From behind him a pop hit was playing through a transistor radio. The counterman turned and snapped it off, though the volume was already turned down. He seemed fidgety about something, and after another minute he came round the counter and stood in the doorway. The blond boy was bent low over the front of the car with the bonnet raised. From where he stood the counterman could read the registration plate if he wanted, and it suddenly struck me that he wanted.

He came back, whistling breathily between his teeth, lifted the counter flap, went through and disappeared into a cubby-hole of an office. The flimsy door closed, but I could hear a sound like a phone being dialled.

I got the flap up and stood behind the door, poking it a little with an index finger. He was talking rapidly.

'. . . yeah, a guy just drove in here with a redhead. I went out and looked at their heap. It's the one you're after, Sheriff . . . you want me to keep them here? Okay, I'll try . . .'

He put the phone up and turned as I pushed the door wide open. His shifty eyes jumped like puffballs on a shooting gallery and his skin went the colour of used dishwater.

'You've been listening to too much radio,' I said. 'Especially police messages.'

He lunged sideways, grabbing at a shotgun propped against the wall below the telephone. I jerked my gun out and put it on him before he could make it.

'Which way is the Sheriff coming?' I said.

'From Cutler Falls, five miles up the road from here, goin' north,' he muttered. He avoided looking at me. I understood that he was lying, but there wasn't the time for an interrogation. I guessed what had happened. Hammer or Logan had put out another call to the law in Winslow in case I showed up there instead of Los Angeles, but it hadn't come until after we'd left. The self-drive bureau would provide the registration number. Then the Winslow police must have put out a message in a local newscast and the counterman had caught it.

'I was only acting as a citizen,' he said.

'Sure. No hard feelings.' I went back and rushed Julie to the car. I was paying the blond kid when he said: 'You're the second car to stop by here in an hour — that makes us busy.'

I smiled meaninglessly and started the motor. He leaned inside and went on: 'We don't get a lot of custom in the mornings. Three guys and a woman it was. She didn't look so well . . .'

I quit revving and shifted the gear back into neutral. 'Do you happen to know which way they went?'

'Why, do you know them?'

'They're friends of ours. We lost track of them in the storm. It looks as if they got lost, too. Which way was it?'

'Waal, they said they was goin' to Tuba City. The main road goes through Oraibi, but there's a cutoff which ud save you some time.'

He told us where it was. I gave him a dollar for himself and he stood back and waved until we were out of sight. A nice lad. Everybody we were meeting was nice. Like hell they were.

We found the cutoff. It was a narrow dirt road plunging between gaunt boulders perched on twin slopes like terracotta sentinels. It would bring us out midway between Oraibi and Tuba City.

The road dipped, swirled round a cliff-like overhang of rock. A jeep was straddled across the road. A man wearing riding boots and a battered Stetson hat stood beside it. He was holding a Winchester repeating rifle of vintage period and looked as if he knew how to handle it.

11

I stopped the car and he moved closer, not hurriedly like a fly cop making a pinch on a city sidewalk. He was used to leisurely, considered movement; the kind of man who would always take his time — unless you crowded him. His face was broad and was tanned by sun and wind and rain and the eyes which looked out from it were pale blue and searching. Although he was a big man, his waistline was slim. He could be any age from fifty to seventy and he had the look of a man it would pay to get along with.

He read the registration plate as he moved in and said: 'I guess you're Shand, Dale Shand. I have to take you into custody, Mr. Shand.'

'What's the charge, Sheriff?'

'I don't rightly know that there is one, Mr. Shand. But we got a radio call to detain you — a call put out by the law in Winslow seemingly at the request of the police in Los Angeles. I understand you're wanted there for questioning.'

'I spoke to Lieutenant Hammer of the Los Angeles Police Department in some detail over the telephone not many hours ago,' I said.

'So? Waal, the message didn't say anything about that — but then, maybe it wouldn't.' He held the long rifle with the barrel pointing at the ground; but I didn't doubt that he could use it very fast if he thought he had to. 'The name is Peel, Sheriff Tom Peel,' he said. He took off his Stetson and nodded to Julie. 'I'm real sorry to trouble you-all, but duty is duty.'

'Are you taking me into custody, too, Sheriff?' asked Julie.

'The message didn't mention you, ma'am, but just to be on the safe side . . . '

'I think the whole thing is ridiculous, Sheriff!'

He smiled. 'That's for the law over in L.A. to decide, I guess,' he said. 'Meanwhile, I'll need to hold you both in custody pending further instructions.' He peered at the car for a moment. 'The best thing will be for the young lady to ride along with me. That way I can be pretty sure of us all getting to town, Mr. Shand.'

'I might make a getaway by myself,' I said.

He eyed me thoughtfully for what seemed like a minute. 'Nope,' he announced at length. 'Nope, I don't figure you for the kind of young fellow who'd leave a woman in the lurch thataway.'

'Thanks.'

'That's how I size you up, Mr. Shand.'

'I mean thanks for calling me young, Sheriff. I'm thirty-nine.'

He chuckled. 'When you get to my age thirty-nine seems real young, son.' He held the door of his jeep open for Julie. 'You drive on ahead, Mr. Shand,' he said. 'Take the second right-hand turn you come to. After that it's a straight run into Cedar Creek.'

There wasn't any way out of it. I drove on, turned where he had said and went down a long, undulating track. After about three miles it widened out, then ran flat and straight into Cedar Creek. A blistered frame building on the main street carried a sign which announced: *Sheriff Tom Peel: Please Enter.*

We went inside. He unlocked a couple of steel cages and bowed us in. 'I'll get us some cawfee, folks,' he said. 'If you're hungry I can fix that, too.'

'I'm not hungry, Sheriff, I'm worried.'

'I reckon you got some cause, son. What you-all done to get on the wrong side of the law?'

'I haven't done anything. Would you care to hear what this is all about?'

He rammed black tobacco in an enormous corncob, tamped it down with the second finger of his right hand and lit it with a blunt kitchen match. The reek was both striking and individual. 'I'm a man with a lot of time,' he said. 'Things are kind of quiet in a little place like this. In fact, some citizens figure I'm paid too much for doin' too little. Yeah, I could be interested.'

He smoked steadily while I told him. Nothing showed on his rugged face. But when I had finished he knocked the dottle out of his pipe and observed thoughtfully:

'Kind of funny what you said about three men and a sick woman in a car. I ain't heard no radio call about them . . . but they hit town not more'n twenty minutes afore you showed up.'

I grabbed the bars of the cage with both hands. 'You mean they're still here?'

'Maybe, maybe not. I can find out.' He went to the door, looked up and down the street, shading his eyes with a vast hand. 'Their heap's outside Jud Ericksson's store,' he said.

Julie uttered a small cry. 'What are you going to do about it?' she demanded.

He pushed his hat back and scratched his grizzled head. 'I don't have no call to arrest them, ma'am. So far as I knows, they ain't done nothing the law wants them for.'

I said: 'Sheriff, you figured me for an honest man. You've got to believe me when I tell you that these men are taking Miss Falaise somewhere against her will.'

'I ain't disputin' what you say, son,' he answered. 'But I got to act legal and right now I don't seem to have no legal status to act upon.'

'And while you're wrestling with your legal conscience they'll be on their way,' stormed Julie.

His open face was troubled. 'Doggone it!' he exploded. 'I can't just walk out on the street and arrest them without cause . . . '

'Wait a minute,' I said. 'Lieutenant Hammer said he was asking the Winslow police to meet these people off a charter flight from Mexico.'

'So you said, son, but I ain't had no official advice about that.'

'The Winslow police must have been preoccupied in catching me,' I said. 'But you've got a telephone, you can call Los Angeles for confirmation of what I say.'

'Yeah, I can do that, Mr. Shand.'

'They might leave town while you're doing it, though. Ask them in for a talk — make any excuse you like, but get them in here.'

'I might go that far. What d'you have in mind?'

'Have you a deputy?'

'Yeah, Jim Corby it is. He'll be along any moment.'

'All right. Keep them talking while the deputy gets through to Los Angeles.'

He nodded and started for the open door. I called: 'Better take your old Winchester.'

'How's that?'

'They might not want to come.'

He grinned and tucked the rifle under the crook of his arm and walked out on to the sunlit street. Minutes passed. They seemed like a small age. Then footsteps and voices sounded. He came back in with two of the men. I had never seen them in my life. A rangy young fellow with a deputy's badge followed.

Peel said: 'Tom, there's a lady in the car, but she ain't so well, so she couldn't come along.' I knew he was saying it just to be saying something.

One of the two, a lantern-jawed man with a flat and expressionless face, snapped: 'What's this all about, Sheriff?'

'Waal now, it's no more'n a friendly talk, I guess,' Peel replied. 'Kind of putting you folks in the picture.'

'Make it quick, we're in a hurry,' the lantern-jawed man said.

'I just wanted to let you folks know there's a couple of road agents on the loose from the county jail,' Peel said imperturbably.

'Oh?'

'Yeah, real bad fellows they are,' Peel went on. He turned to the deputy and said: 'Jim — you'd better put that call through. I've wrote down the number.' He passed a slip of paper over.

Corby went across the floor and into a rear office. The first of the two men said harshly: 'Thanks for the warning, Sheriff, but I guess we can take care of ourselves if the need arises.'

'Maybe, but you got a sick lady to think of, Mister . . . ?'

'Smith.'

'Vacationing in these parts, Mr. Smith?' asked Peel innocently.

'Just passing through.' The man who had lied about his name shifted irritably. 'Well, if that's all, I guess we'll be on our way and — '

He stopped suddenly. From the rear office Corby's voice came loud enough to hear. A hardrock pioneer voice you could hear through the slammed door of a bank vault. 'Los Angeles City Police? I want to speak to Captain Logan or Lieutenant Hammer about . . . '

Sheriff Peel made one mistake. He turned. Smith laughed, a harsh rasp of sound. A gun jumped into his hand. He backed towards the door, his eyes glittering. Peel moved so fast the movement was no more than a blur, but he had already lost the vital time. Before he could use his rifle Smith had fired a .32 Colt Woodsman. The bullet tore through the Sheriff's thigh and he went down with a thud. The street door banged shut as Corby rushed from the rear office.

On the floor Peel roared: 'It's only a flesh wound . . . get after them, Jim!'

The deputy went through the door with his gun out. Two shots exploded simultaneously. Corby spun completely round, then dived to the boardwalk. Out on the dusty street a car screamed through its gears and was gone.

For a moment nothing happened. Then running footsteps sounded. Someone picked Corby up and carried him inside.

He was as dead as a codfish on a marble slab. Sheriff Peel crawled across the floor. He put a hand in a pocket, took out a bunch of keys and tossed them in the cage to me.

'You're free, son,' he said. 'You and the young lady is free as air.'

'I'll get the local doc, Sheriff,' I said.

'Nope, he'll come anyways, son.' He winced and went on. 'You get after them killers . . . you're sworn-in as a deputy . . . '

12

I drove west on the narrow road with a deputy's badge pinned to my shirt. A white Cadillac, a blue Plymouth, three battered old heaps and a farm truck followed like an ill-assorted motorcade bristling with men and guns. Sheriff Tom Peel was well-liked in Cedar Creek.

We picked up the main route and went fast down a long, straight section, but there was no sign of the escaping car. I flagged the Caddy down and the driver passed the signal on. He was a large, untidy man with a face which looked as if it had been hewn from the rock in the Grand Canyon.

'They cain't have got that far ahead,' he said. 'We must've lost them somewheres.'

'I guess so, Mr. Bartley. We passed five intersections in the last few miles. The car must have gone down one of them. Where do they lead?'

'They're just small country roads serving pretty isolated communities — but them coyotes could use any one of them as a detour and finally make Tuba City.'

'I see. The best thing would be for us to split up, taking different routes.'

He nodded his shaggy head. 'We'll do that!' He barked orders and the vehicles made a variety of slow turns, heading back the way we had come. I took the first of the five side roads, with Bartley on our tail. It was little more than a rutted lane, winding through arable land at first and then drifting between wooded foot-hills.

We had gone five miles when Julie said: 'Mr. Bartley's stopped. He's waving at us.'

I braked, poked my head out and Bartley shouted: 'Sump'n wrong with my car . . . ignition trouble, I think.'

'You can ride with us.'

'Nope, I'll fix it. I know plenty about cars, this one in particular. I'll catch you up.'

'All right.' I drove on again. Julie had

taken a comb out and was doing something to her hair. She managed to be dishevelled and intriguing simultaneously. Shand merely looked dishevelled.

'I want a shower, a change of clothes and some sleep,' she said.

'I want a razor.'

'You look fine, Dale.'

'You're just being kind to an ageing man.'

'Ageing? At thirty-nine?'

'I feel like ninety-nine.'

'You're a gorgeous man and I love you madly.' She wrinkled her nose and went on: 'Everything's crazy. I can't really believe it's happening. All my well-ordered civilized life seems like something left behind in a vanished world. It's different for you, you're used to having adventures.'

'Some, but not this kind of adventure.'

She trembled. 'You mean that poor boy who was shot . . . it's horrible . . . '

'No, I didn't mean that. I've seen men killed before.'

'I . . . suppose so. To me it's something you read about in the newspapers and

you think it can never happen to you — '
She stopped.

I said: 'That's it — it could happen to *you*. These men are killers. I don't like your being here.'

'I can't get out and walk.'

'No . . . '

'And I wouldn't.'

'If we get within sighting distance of their car, you duck right down and stay out of sight,' I said.

She moved herself until she touched me. 'I'm unwashed, mussed-up, my face looks a wreck and I'm petrified with fright and I'm loving it,' she said. 'What did you mean about not having had this kind of adventure?'

'Exactly that. I do my work mostly in cities, I'm not accustomed to the wide-open spaces.' I was staring through the windscreen as I spoke. In the next instant I was swerving violently across the narrow road. There was a high keening sound and a rifle bullet hit a rock on the hillside and ricocheted off.

'Down — get down on the floor, Julie!'

She ducked as I drove between two

massive trees with about a couple of inches to spare on either side. Another whine, another bullet, but I knew he couldn't see us now from where he was shooting, which was on the summit of the opposite slope. I had seen the glint of his sights a split second before he triggered it the first time.

I got my automatic out, not that it was likely to be much use at that range. A figure appeared like a black dot on the hillside, then another. I put the car into low gear and carefully slid it forward between the big trees. A trail opened out, little more than the width of the car, but you could drive on it. The trail dipped, ran between more trees, flowed across uneven land, round a couple of boulder-strewn slopes and suddenly dived to a valley.

There was a small blue-water lake in the middle of the valley. Trees fringed one side of the lake and in a clearing stood a rambling log-built house. A veranda spanned the front of the house and in the middle of the veranda a woman sat in a rocking chair, moving with a slow easy rhythm. I drove round the edge of the lake and stopped.

The woman looked down at us from an old, old face wrinkled as a crab-apple, coppered layers deep by the Arizona sun and topped by a mass of wild grey and yellowed hair like a mad haystack. She looked at least a hundred, but was probably not more than eighty years old; and her eyes were ageless. She wore a shapeless flowing black dress which looked as if it had come West with the wagon trains, and was holding a bent clay pipe between four yellowed teeth, two up and two down.

'Hiya, friends,' she called. Her voice was a sandpapered contralto, sharp enough to slice bread on, but amiable.

I took Julie's hand and we walked up the three steps to the veranda. Nobody fired more rifles. Perhaps we had eluded them. Perhaps not.

The old, old woman eyed Julie appraisingly. 'It's nice to see young folks,' she said. 'I don't see many in this neck of the woods. Come to think of it, I don't see much of any kind of folks.'

I started to say something, but the old woman went on, still looking at Julie: 'You're real pretty, honey. Any man would be mighty proud to take you into his bed.'

Julie flushed. The old woman chuckled. 'No offence. That was meant as a compliment. Yessir, a real compliment.'

'Well, thank you, then.'

'It's a long whiles since anybody could say that about me,' the old woman mused. 'About thirty years, I guess.' She took the clay pipe from her only teeth and spat on the veranda. 'You here on a vacation?'

'Not exactly,' I said. 'Somebody just tried to shoot us.'

'You don't say?' She didn't seem alarmed. 'That must've been them shots I heard just now. Kind of distant they was, but I heard 'em. Yessir, I kin hear real well. Who's trying to kill you?'

'It's a somewhat long and complicated story, Mrs . . . ?'

She chuckled again. 'Not Mrs., son. I ain't never been wed. Not legal, I mean.'

'Oh?'

'Nope. I've had seven unofficial husbands and more lovers than a hound dawg has fleas, but that was a long time back. Fourteen children, all gone from here. Some in Texas, some in New Mexico and my youngest in Noo York. The name is McGarritty, Ma McGarritty. Howdy!'

She put out a veined hand. It felt hard as a rock. 'You look like a good man, son,' she offered. 'Yessir, a real good man, and they's mighty hard to find. Always was — and I should know. Only one of my men was anything but a no-good layabout.' She eyed me directly and added: 'You want to take cover in my house?'

'I don't want you to be in any danger, Ma. Just tell us the quickest way out of here.'

'Danger,' she said. 'Why not? That's sump'n I could use a little of. What's your names?'

I told her. She cackled. 'Dale and Julie — powerful pretty names. You treat him right, honey. This here is a good man with a fine strong frame. If I was a young girl again I'd run a brand on him afore he tried to escape.' She sucked noisily on the clay pipe. 'This danger now. How soon is it goin' to show up?'

'I don't know that it is, but it's possible. I guess we'll be on our way.'

She quit swinging to and fro in the rocker and stood up. She was tall, a good five feet eight inches, and stout with it, though you didn't especially notice it because of her height. What you really saw was the lined and seamed face — the unclouded eyes with their piercing black pupils, the strong fleshed nose and the intricate network of fine lines crossing and re-crossing her face. A used face, a face of character, a face that had seen happiness and sadness, fulfilment and despair and had triumphed over them all.

'You stay right here!' she shouted. 'If some pesky rattlers is bent on a little shootin' I aim to be right in there pitchin' . . . '

If I still had objections I didn't have time to utter them. A car was rumbling down the steep trail, not yet in sight. The execution squad was arriving.

'Inside, the pair of you!' bawled Ma McGarritty.

We had no choice now. We went inside and she slammed the door shut, turned a key which looked big enough to lock-up the moated castle and swung a massive iron bar across the door. The car stopped. There was a long pause, then footsteps and voices sounded in the distance.

Ma grinned and took down a shotgun and clipped cartridges in and handed it to me. She got two more from a corner of the big littered room and looked across at Julie.

'Kin you shoot straight, honey?'

Julie shook her head. 'I can't shoot — straight or any other way, I never handled a gun in my life,' she said.

'Your eddication has been kind of neglected,' snorted Ma. 'Maybe you kin re-load for us, though?'

'I think so — I watched you do it.'

'They's a box of cartridges right by you and three more shotguns . . . git loading!'

'What are we going to do — let fly through an open window?' I inquired.

'Hell, no.' Ma pointed a finger at the

145

wall on either side of the window. Medium-sized holes had been drilled in it. 'I put them in ten years ago when I first started living alone, just in case I ever needed to protect myself.'

I thrust a gun barrel through one of the slots. It was big enough to take the gun and sight it. The three men outside looked like sitting ducks. They started closing in on the house, fanning out.

The one who had pulled a gun in the Sheriff's office was in the middle. He said: 'They must be inside, their car's here. The guy who was driving it was in that Sheriff's place — in one of the cages. Yet now he's out looking for us.' He laughed harshly. 'It's my guess he's Shand.'

One of the other men said: 'You mean the gumshoe we got a message about from Frank Malone?'

'It must be. That Sheriff must've taken him in, and then let him out after us.'

'We don't know that for certain. Why risk hanging around here?'

'Shut up! We're going in.' Smith raised his voice and yelled: 'If you're not out with your hands up in five seconds we're coming for you . . . '

Ma let out a dry chuckle and curled a finger round the trigger. A torrent of buckshot sprayed the loose soil at their feet. They jumped clean off the ground, then started running back. Smith turned and fired at the window. Glass splintered into the room.

'So you want trouble, huh?' Ma said. 'Let 'em have it, son!'

Smith was down on one knee, aiming again. I fired a deliberate near miss, but he toppled right over, howling. Ma was spraying buckshot all over the place.

'Doggone it, them coyotes'll be fuller of holes than a colander,' she roared. 'Gimme another gun, honey!'

But it was too late. All three had crawled, hopped and jigged into the shelter of the trees. Ma bellowed rage and raked the whole scene with a continuous crossfire. The only thing she hit this time was the car we had come in — one end of it sank gracefully into the grass, the nearside rear tyre cut to ribbons.

I looked through the smashed window.

Smith was kneeling on the ground with blood trickling from his hands, but one of them still held a gun.

'Shed the heater, mug,' I called. 'If I have to fire again you get the full charge.'

In fact, I thought it would be less than easy at that range, but he climbed painfully to his feet and left his automatic pistol on the ground. The others were moaning and nursing an assortment of small wounds. Ma came alongside me grinning, a still-smoking gun held out from her body.

'Kin I give 'em just one more peppering, Dale?' she pleaded.

'They're almost out of range,' I said.

'I kin walk out on the veranda.'

'Next time you might kill somebody, Ma.'

' 'Pears like you just made a sensible proposition,' she said. 'Tarnation, I ain't had so much fun since my last man broke a leg chasing a serving wench and him in his sixty-ninth year.'

'Stand guard over them, Ma, while I find their car. They left it back up the trail. It can't be far.'

'I'll do that, son, and they better not try any fancy pants,' said Ma cosily.

Julie came with me. We went round one end of the lake and started up the trail through the trees. 'They must have left it a long way back,' she suggested.

'We'll find it in a minute … ' I stopped. Out of sight in the distance a motor sounded, then a jarring sound like a crashed low gear without benefit of synchromesh. I left Julie standing and raced madly up the slope. The trees thinned slightly. I could see the trail as it wound upwards and curved. I could also see the rear fender of the car as it made the first turn and vanished.

'Annette … Annette … come back!' Even as I yelled the words I knew it was too late.

13

We went back to the log house. Ma had locked all three in one of the rooms. 'They ain't hurt, not real bad,' she announced. 'Anyways, I'll fix 'em up temporary until we kin get the doc, which is more'n they deserve, I guess. Did you find the car and the lady you was looking for?'

'She must have recovered, at least enough to drive. She's gone and we've no way of going after her.'

I looked at the ripped tyre. 'By the time we've changed a wheel she could be anywhere. Until now we knew which direction the car was taking . . . '

'Waal,' replied Ma comfortably, 'if the lady has got clean away on her own it's all right, isn't it? She's safe from this bunch of no-goods.'

'For the time being.'

'How's that?'

'These three men are part of a crime

organization. There are others.'

'Yeah, but they don't know where to start looking now, Dale.'

'They've got agents planted in a lot of places. They'll pick her up again in time.'

Ma stacked her shotgun against a wall. 'Not jest yet, though,' she said. 'So you ain't pressed for time. I'm sorry I shot your tyre, though.'

'That's all right, you didn't intend it.'

'I guess I was a mite carried away with enthusiasm, Dale. I was swinging that old shotgun in a kind of semicircle.'

'So I noticed. The thing is where do I get a replacement cover? We'd better have one. We can't risk carrying on with no spare.'

'Why not call the nearest service depôt and have them bring one out?' suggested Julie innocently.

Ma was pushing rank tobacco in her clay pipe. 'Ain't got no phone, honey,' she said. 'I never did hold with them noo-fangled notions.'

'A car then?'

'A horse and buggy I got, but the horse is limping a little. I've doctored him up some, but he won't be fit till morning at the earliest.'

'Then we'll have to walk into town,' I growled.

'Walk? Doggone it, the nearest village is all of fifteen miles from here,' objected Ma.

'But these three men need a doctor, don't they?' said Julie.

'I done told you they's all right. I'm going to fix 'em up. They only got a few pellets in their dirty hides and we kin fetch Doc Sigsbee in the buggy first thing in the morning.'

'We'd better take a look at them,' I said. 'I suppose you took their guns away?'

'First thing I did, afore looking at their itty-bitty cuts, Dale.' She unlocked the door.

The man who had called himself Smith was sitting on a bed which looked as if it hadn't been slept in since William Jennings Bryan made his speech in the Dayton monkey trial. The others sat around in hard-backed chairs.

Smith rasped: 'We need a doc. You

can't keep us here.'

I didn't answer. I just stood there with a gun while Ma went to work. She took seven pellets from their hands, faces and legs and cleaned the small wounds with something that smelled like horse liniment and probably was, judging by the agonized yelps.

When she was through I said: 'Where were you taking Annette Falaise?'

Three pairs of eyes looked at me without expression, without anything you could put a name to. Smith was a thickset man in his early forties with a heavy sensual face and a nose like an eagle's beak. It seemed probable that his real name was Italian or Sicilian. I knew that none of them was going to talk and that nothing I was likely to do would make them. The price of squealing would be a kangaroo court and the issuing of contracts for their liquidation. They would take their chance with me rather than face the certainty of being dropped in a river with a fruit machine round their feet and their intestinal tract posthumously ice-picked to stop their bodies floating to the surface.

I shrugged. 'All right, we'll turn you over to the law.'

Smith stared with his flat, emptied eyes. 'You got nothing on us, Shand. We came here to pay a call and you and this old crone started shooting and — ' He broke off suddenly, as if another thought had come to him.

'You'll have to do better than that,' I said. 'You kidnapped Annette Falaise.'

One of the others, a skinny number with a cleft chin, said: 'She was sick. We was taking her to hospital, that's all.'

Ma, who was washing her hands in a bucket, said: 'You ain't taking her no place now, she's beat it in your jalopy.'

A muscle twitched like a reflex on Smith's heavy face, but his eyes had gone uneasy. I knew what was troubling him.

'You nearly overlooked something else,' I said. 'One or two of you shot and killed the Deputy Sheriff. I guess that'll be more than enough.'

Smith's face was ashen. One of the others started to say something, but he

154

snarled: 'Clam up! The Organization'll spring us.'

'I wouldn't bet on it,' I said and banged the door on them.

We went back into the living-room. Ma stirred a vast stew-pot. 'I guess you folks must be hungry,' she said.

'Very — but we'd like to wash-up first,' said Julie.

'Ain't got no bathroom, honey — you'll have to use a tin tub.'

I looked out at the lake. The water was calm and shining under the full moon. 'I'm going for a swim,' I said.

'I'll come with you, Dale.'

I grinned. 'It'll have to be in the altogether.'

A cackle erupted from Ma. 'Why not?' she said. 'You both look like you got nothing to be ashamed of seeing.'

I went in first, gasping at the impact of the cool lakewater. But in a few minutes it seemed almost tepid. I swam far out. Julie came after me, cleaving the surface with a steady crawl. Her long coppery hair floated behind her.

We lay almost motionless in the water,

hands joined. I started humming an old number from way back.

Julie said suddenly: 'I know that tune. It's *Rockin' Chair* . . . '

'Yes, Hoagy Carmichael wrote it.'

'So he did — *Stardust*, too.'

'That's right — back in 1927. He's been collecting around twelve thousand dollars in royalties every year since.'

'How do you know that?'

'A newspaperman I know interviewed him some years ago and Hoagy told him. Incidentally, he wrote *Rockin' Chair* in his head while swimming in a lake after an all-night session on home-brew in a log cabin owned by a very old woman who had a rocking chair.'

Julie laughed. 'History repeating itself — except that you haven't had a poetic inspiration, have you?'

'Not about writing a musical hit.' I slid an arm round her cool naked body. She laughed again and wriggled free.

Then we swam back to the shore, side by side. Julie wound a big towel round her and darted inside. 'There's another towel, it looks like a horse towel,' she called. 'Make yourself decent before you come in.'

'I don't think Ma would be offended if I didn't,' I said.

We were dressed and eating hash with home-baked bread and applejack cider on the side when Ma said: 'They's a car comin' . . . '

I got up and went to the door. A jeep rumbled to a stop and Sheriff Tom Peel climbed out. 'Hell,' he said, 'it's you!'

'How on earth did you know where to find us, Sheriff?'

'I didn't, son. I wasn't looking for you. The doc fixed me up and I just drove out on the off chance of picking up the trail. I couldn't see a sign of you or the others and decided to stop-off at Ma McGarritty's place. Howdy, Ma!'

'Howdy, Tom.' Ma's bulk loomed in the doorway. 'Come right in. You got the gen'ral look of a man who could use a drink.'

He tramped in and Ma added: 'What did you-all want to see me about?'

'I wondered if maybe you'd seen some of the boys who went out with Dale, that's all.' He looked round at us inquiringly and I told him what had happened.

'You mean you got them ornery critters right here?'

'In a bedroom, all locked up and bandaged up.'

'Doggone it, son, you're the best deputy I ever did have!' he exploded.

'Ma had plenty to do with it — and Julie. We did the shooting while Julie re-loaded.'

'I'm mighty grateful, Dale.' His face clouded. 'They done killed Jim Corby,' he said harshly. 'And Jim only wed a year and leaving a young widow seven months with child.' He fingered his rifle, then put it down. 'No, I ain't gonna shoot them,' he said. 'The law'll take its course.'

'I hope so, Tom.'

'What d'you mean, you hope so?'

'These men are members of a criminal syndicate called The Organization. They'll get a smart lawyer.'

'So? I'll tell you sump'n, son — they'll get a smart trial, too, in these parts. Folks round here won't be in no mood to listen to some shyster lawyer from the big city. The jury'll do their duty on the testimony — and it's conclusive.'

'You've got witnesses?'

He nodded. 'Two of the gang fired the shots which killed Jim and they was seen.'

'That ought to be conclusive enough. You can drive them back into town when you leave.'

'I'll do that, son. What about the sick lady they was taking away unlawfully?'

'She recovered sufficiently to drive off in their car while they were trying to break in here.'

His eyes widened. 'So you don't know where she's gone?'

'No.'

'Waal, she's safe from them, anyways.'

'But not from The Organization as such. Still, she's safe for the time being. I'd still like to warn her, though.'

'I can understand that, son — but it seems like you don't know where to start looking.' He thought for a moment, then went on: 'I can put out a radio call from the office. If we pick up a clue it's yours. You can drive back with me . . . '

'I'll drive 'em out in the buggy first thing in the morning,' Ma said. 'They's kind of tuckered out and needing their rest.'

'All right,' I said.

Tom Peel had been gone nearly an hour when Ma yawned and announced: 'I'm catching-up on my sleep. You'd better do the same.' She grinned. 'The bedroom's right across the hallway. Have another drink afore you turn in . . . but only one.'

Julie looked at her retreating figure. 'I love Ma, she's a terribly real person,' she said.

'Yes.'

'What did she mean about not having more than one more drink?'

I laughed. 'That's Ma's way of issuing a small warning.'

'A warning — about what?'

'Alcohol stimulates the biological urge while denying the means of its gratification.'

She looked at me for a long moment. Then she took the stone jar of applejack from me and said: 'In that case, you're not going to risk even one more drink.'

I picked her up and carried her through the door and across the hallway. In the room there was an enormous double bed. It was canopied all round.

'Complete privacy guaranteed,' murmured Julie.

'I don't think Ma would sneak a look, anyway,' I said.

14

It was twenty minutes after eight o'clock next morning when Sheriff Tom Peel drove up in his jeep, climbed down and walked up to the veranda with a slight limp. I was sitting in Ma's rocking chair smoking a pipe. Ma was washing the breakfast dishes with Julie. A scene of tranquil domesticity.

'How's the thigh this morning, Tom?'

'Slight flesh wound, like I said, son, and still a mite stiff. But it'd take more'n that to keep me out of things.' There was a wicker chair next to me and he sank gratefully into it. 'I've brought you a new tyre for your heap,' he said.

'That's nice of you. How much do I owe?'

He told me and I paid him. 'I suppose you and Miss Julie will be leaving?' he ventured.

'I'm afraid so, Sheriff.'

He filled his pipe from a crumpled

oilskin pouch and said: 'Why not stop on here, son? I need a new full-time deputy and I kind of like you.'

'The feeling is mutual, Tom, but . . . '

He looked directly at me. 'This is a great country, Dale. You'll not find a better climate. Fishing, shooting, clean air and sun . . . you could make yourself a good life here. Why go back to one of them cities?'

'New York in my case.'

'I visited there one time,' he said. 'In the Fall of 1929, just before the Depression. I only stayed three nights. I felt kind of cramped.'

'It's worse now.'

'I guess so. All them automobiles and folks hurrying to and fro like they was a million ants. I used to wonder where they was all going and if they ever stopped to ask themselves what it was all about.'

'Most of them are just trying to get by and worrying about the bills and whether they can afford the repayments on a new car.'

'I never bought nothing I couldn't put the cash down for, son. Mind you, even out here some folks do, but they look kind of troubled in mind.'

'What I meant was that the pace of life in big cities is bound up with the daily act of making a living.'

'I guess so — but there must be better ways. A man needs to make a living here, just the same, but he don't have to wear his health down in order to do it.' He stabbed his pipe stem at the air and resumed: 'You're one of them private detectives, according to the message we picked up. What did you do before that?'

I told him and he grinned. 'Just the right training for a real good deputy if he has what I judge to be the right pers'nal qualities — and I judge you got them, son. How do you like it out here in Arizona?'

'I like it fine, Tom.'

'You could make yourself a good life here.'

'Yes, I think I could.'

'Then why not do it? You could marry Miss Julie and have kids.'

'I'm not sure she wants to marry, Tom.'

'All women want to marry, son. It's as

natural as night following day.' He eyed me reflectively. 'Maybe you're the reluctant one?'

'It's possible. I'm getting past the age at which a man marries readily.'

'Could be, though I've known men do it in their fifties. But married or single, there's a job waiting for you . . . and one day you'd be Sheriff.'

'Now you're fishing with live bait,' I grinned.

He chuckled. 'You could call it that. It's true just the same.'

'I'll have to go, Tom,' I said seriously. 'I've still got to find Miss Falaise.'

'You figure they'll keep looking for her, even though we've got them three varmints in custody?'

'Yes. They're just hired torpedoes and expendable. There'll be others to take their place.'

'But you still don't know where to look for her.'

'I'll have to try.'

'I wouldn't wish to stop you, Dale. I'd just like to think you'd come back here with Miss Julie when it's all over.'

'You mean for good?'

'I'm offering you the job, son,' he answered quietly.

'It's tempting,' I said. 'But I'm less than certain that I'd fit. I'm accustomed to cities.'

'You could soon get unaccustomed, a man like you.' He sighed. 'I wouldn't have let you stay on here immediately, anyways . . . '

'Why, what's happened?'

'I know where Miss Falaise has gone,' he said simply.

'You could have told me before, Tom.'

'There's no hurry, not for the ten minutes I've used up talking with you, Dale. That's one of the things you learn out here — how to take things unhurriedly.' He fired another match for his pipe, drew on it and said: 'A car like the one she drove off in was left on a parking lot in Tuba City. I did some telephoning before coming out here and a clerk at the railroad depôt said a woman answering to her description bought a one-way ticket to Las Vegas.'

'Thanks,' I said. I started to get up.

'It ain't conclusive, Dale. It could be somebody else.'

'You don't really think that, Tom.'

'Nope. I guess the chances are it's her. I was kind of acting cautious. A man like me don't jump to conclusions very easy. But if it was her what d'you aim to do?'

'Start driving to Las Vegas,' I said.

'It's a big town, Vegas,' he mused. 'A big, noisy, brawling kind of town. How will you start looking when you get there?'

'I'll think of ways.'

'Yeah,' he said slowly. 'Yeah, I guess you'll do just that. I . . .'

Julie came out on the veranda looking wonderful. 'Why, Sheriff Peel,' she cried. 'I thought I heard your voice. What brings you out so early?'

'Several things, Miss Julie. I been trying to persuade Dale to stay on here as Deputy Sheriff.'

She glanced at me. A long smiling glance with a question-mark at the end of it.

'The Sheriff thinks I ought to settle here — you, too.'

'Well?'

'He also thinks he knows where Annette's gone,' I said. 'It's virtually certain she got to Tuba City and bought a railroad ticket to Las Vegas.'

Ma thrust her vast bulk through the doorway. She was standing with her hands splayed on her hips. 'Vegas!' she roared. 'Who but a passel of layabouts ever wanted to get within a hundred miles of that godforsaken, festering stewpot?'

'The Las Vegas Chamber of Commerce wouldn't like to hear that remark, Ma.'

'The hell with what the Las Vegas Chamber of Commerce ud like to hear,' replied Ma amiably. 'You mark my words — no good ever came of tangling with a place like that. I should know. I went there once with my third — no, my fourth man it was.'

'And took a dislike to it on the spot?'

'I lost fifty bucks at the faro table.'

'Ah!' I said feelingly.

'It wasn't just losing the fifty,' Ma retorted. 'Though, mind you, it hurt some — especially as Calvin never earned an honest dime in his life and only fixed a leak in the roof if I got after him with a hatchet.'

'You don't seem to have had much luck in your emotional life, Ma,' said Julie.

'Only with one of them and he was a good man — like Dale here.' Ma turned her piercing black eyes on me. 'And now I suppose you're rushing off to Vegas to find that missing young woman?'

'I must do it, Ma. She's still in danger.'

Tom Peel stood up and put out a hand. 'Good luck to you, son,' he said. 'But when you've done what you feel is right, think over that offer.'

I almost took it there and then. I thought of the life I live in New York; the loneliness, the rich clients made arrogant by too much money, the poor clients made timid by fear of the next bill, the shabby boredom of much of the work I do, the other times when boredom suddenly ends on the threshold of violence, the chance that some night I could go out and never come back except in an ambulance bound for the morgue. Why do I do it? Partly because I drifted into it, but mainly because it gives me the sensation of individual freedom in a world in which the area of freedom is being constantly eroded. An Arizona deputy might be shot at — in fact, I had been shot at — but he would have a sense of individuality more satisfying than anything New York or Chicago or Los Angeles could give. A sense of belonging, too — that sense of integration and continuing purpose which is one of the first things you lose in a great urban community. But I had to find Annette Falaise.

We left less than an hour later. Sheriff Tom Peel and Ma McGarritty stood side by side on the veranda watching us go. Julie waved. When she turned back her eyes were moist.

'They're wonderful people, real people,' she said.

'Yes. Do you think I'd make a deputy sheriff?'

'It's not what *I* think, Dale. How about you?'

'I don't know. I like the idea, though.'

She laughed. 'Dale Shand, the private eye from the big city, with ten years of

Western sun on his face, a Stetson hat, a slow drawl and riding around in a jeep with a Winchester on the back seats and a Colt forty-five in a gunbelt. You could do it, you know.'

'I'm not sure.'

'Oh, you could do it fine. You're not a city slicker, not really. How long have you lived in New York?'

'It must be fifteen years.'

'And you're still not a natural city dweller,' she said. 'I can tell it.'

'I was born and raised in a small town in the Middle West. I dare say I still have something of that left.'

'Oh, yes. Nobody ever wholly losses the formative influences of childhood. But you're not going back to Arizona?'

'I'm going back to see Sheriff Tom Peel and Ma McGarritty one more time.'

'I'll come with you, Dale,' she said.

15

We went north from Tuba City, up through Marble Canyon and Jakob Lake, moving close to the Utah state line, then swinging west through Mesquite and Dry Lake and on down to Las Vegas. A long hot drive with a lot of undemanding talk and many miles in which neither of us spoke. Sometimes we changed places, sometimes we stopped.

It was night when we finally hit Vegas. The place was jammed. Ma McGarritty's description fitted all right. It looked like a neon-lit Gehenna of noise and greed. Noise everywhere, with the keynote set by the gigantic amplified voice booming 'Howdy, pardners' with a sort of macabre heartiness; greed on the sweating faces of the men and women, whether on the sidewalks, playing the gaming tables or working the massed banks of one-armed bandits with the sullen desperation of slaves in some factory system of unimaginable horror. An ocean of faces, all different and yet somehow the same. Few looked even remotely happy.

We checked-in at one of the smaller hotels. I picked up a telephone and called a number. A male voice answered, a flat voice with much less expression than a tombstone on Boot Hill. The voice went away and another came on the line. A deep, urbane voice.

'Shand! What are you doing way out West?'

'Looking for a little information. I thought you might be able to help.'

'That depends what it is,' he said. 'Suppose you come over?'

I hung up and collected Julie. 'We're going to see the guy I told you about on the way . . .'

'The Englishman they call Lord John Ballard?'

'That's right. Of course, he's not in the British peerage. The only time he was a guest of Her Majesty was in Dartmoor, a four-year stretch for embezzlement and falsification of accounts. He got the nickname out here because of his English accent.'

'I don't see how an ex-convict can help you, Dale.'

'So far as I know, Ballard has no criminal record over here. He stays on the right side of the law — technically, anyway. I knew him in New York. He came out West about four years ago. He knows this town and there's just a chance that he may know about Annette and the connection with The Organization.'

'I suppose so, but he might not be willing to talk about it, especially if . . . ' She shrugged.

'You mean if he's involved with The Organization himself? I'd doubt that. Ballard is a lone wolf and runs a small but plushy gambling club. Besides, he owes me a small debt of gratitude.'

'Oh? You never said anything about that.'

'I saved his life, as a matter of fact. Somebody went for a gun when Ballard was unarmed. I knocked it out of the guy's hand before he could fire it.'

'I still don't see how Mr. Ballard can help us,' she said.

'We'll find out, Julie.'

Ballard's place was not far from The Sands. A commissionaire with a broad careful face which looked as if it had been around smiled a broad, careful and utterly meaningless smile. I poked a business card at him, the one without the crossed guns rampant, and he bore it away. When he came back the smile was near genuine warmth as it was ever likely to get.

He led us through a crimson door and down a short cream-walled corridor to another crimson door with *Lord John Ballard* inscribed on it in letters that looked like solid gold and possibly were.

Ballard rose from behind an inlaid eighteenth-century desk with a gold-tipped leather-bound blotter and a gold-and-leather pen set. He was pushing fifty and had a little more weight than when we last met, but he was still a handsome man with his strong tanned face, clear blue eyes and thick dark hair tentatively routed with grey. He wore a dinner suit which suggested the craftsmanship of Savile Row, simple pearl shirt studs and plain gold cufflinks.

'You didn't mention that you were bringing a lady, my dear chap,' he said. 'Not that I am cavilling.' His eyes flicked to Julie and back to me. 'Drink?'

'Thanks.'

'Scotch, of course,' he smiled. He glanced again at Julie.

'Miss Julie Arden,' I said.

'I'd prefer brandy,' Julie remarked.

He made the drinks, peeled the band off an eight-inch cigar and looked it over closely as if suspecting nuclear radiation. Then he lifted his eyes and said: 'What do you want me to tell you, Shand?'

'I'm looking for a former singer named Annette Falaise. It's a matter of some urgency. There's some reason to think that she may be in Las Vegas.'

'Annette Falaise . . . ' He spoke the name thoughtfully. 'I remember her. A very good singer indeed. She sang here once, not in my club, but here in Vegas. Her last professional appearance, wasn't it?'

'You don't need me to tell you that,' I said.

'No, of course not, I was just recalling circumstances. She walked out on her contract to marry Dino Carelli. The law caught up with him and after that she was through.' He blew a thin spiral of cigar smoke and said: 'What makes you think she may be here?'

I didn't answer directly. Instead, I said: 'Will you first tell me one thing?'

'Again, that depends what it is, my dear fellow.' He looked down the line of the cigar and went on: 'No — I'll answer to the best of my ability and without reservations. I owe you that much, more in fact. What's the question?'

'Are you in any way linked with a new syndicate which calls itself The Organization?'

His eyes had a sudden wary look in them. 'No,' he said. 'Will that do?'

I nodded and told him everything. It took nearly ten minutes. The cigar burned down a little between his ringless fingers, unsmoked. Finally, he said: 'The Organization is a new factor out here. We know something about it.'

'How many are we?'

'People, Shand, just people.' He smiled his smooth, urbane smile.

'You mean people in business, the men who control gambling in Vegas?'

'They're naturally interested in any new development,' Ballard answered. 'Specifically, any development that might have an inconvenient potential. What else would you expect?'

'Nothing less than that. But The Organization is still in a formative stage.'

'That's true, old chap. But our information is that they're getting ready to make a move.' He made his wide smile again, not quite so urbane now. 'Other chaps will be ready, too, Shand.'

'Who's representing The Organization here — do you know that?'

'We're not really sure, though we have some names. One thing we do know is that none of the names previously linked with The Syndicate are in it. Actually, we don't have firm evidence about any new men trying to do a Buggsy Siegel act in California or here in Nevada.'

Siegel was before my time, but I knew about him. He moved out West back in 1937, muscled-in on the motion picture business through control of the film extras, and later took $25,000 a month from the wire service racket in Las Vegas alone. But his lofty insistence on running the California wire service as his own personal property was too much for The Syndicate. Even Jack Dragna deserted him. A few weeks later the Bug was hit — blown clean out of his chair in the ornate living-room of his girl friend's home where he was sitting, rather indiscreetly, against an open window.

This was the heyday of Frank Carbo and Champ Segal, of Kid Reles and Big Greenie — and, above all, of Buggsy Siegel and Jack Dragna, who was once labelled the Al Capone of Los Angeles. If The Organization had recruited latter-day executives of matching calibre, California was heading for trouble. I said as much.

Ballard grinned. 'We have our eyes open and our ears to the ground, you know,' he replied.

'What's that mean, in practical terms?'

'Just that we are on to a number of new faces in town.'

'Names — do you know their names?'

'Willie Kapete, Dandy Jim Longman, Fred Murrah, Caesar Vuolo, Joey Massano . . .'

'Imports from Sicily,' I said dryly.

'Possibly, though more probably they're second generation, born in America. Longman isn't Sicilian, anyway. He's a battered onetime heavyweight from Seattle and still carries the trademark, a cauliflower ear.'

'They sound like a bunch of torpedoes.'

'Some, perhaps. But we've had no trouble. They're just fellows we're keeping an eye on, as you might say. I gather you have never heard of them?'

'No, the only apparently authoritative name I know is Frank Malone . . .' I stopped because Ballard's face had suddenly lost its smiling blandness.

'Malone,' he said. 'We've heard of him. We thought he was in New York. He most certainly isn't here. Where did you run across him?'

'I told you about being taken to a house in Beverly Hills. Malone was one of the men who took me there.'

'I see. Then he must be organizing something in Los Angeles, possibly in Hollywood as well.'

'Could be, but he wasn't the boss. That would be the man I never saw, the voice over the microphone.'

'Describe his voice to me, Shand. I might know him.'

'I can't give an authentic impersonation. It was a flat sort of voice, almost totally devoid of expression — but that may have been assumed.'

'Any mannerisms?'

'I remember one, though it's a small thing. He had a habit of reiterating the Italian word *amico* . . . '

I stopped again. This time Ballard's face was tight and when he answered it was in a voice you could use to strip paint. 'Johnny Cassatta!'

'I don't know him,' I said.

'Nobody does, old boy — nobody outside a chosen circle of intimates. The name is almost certainly false. But it's known that Cassatta has this one vocal idiosyncracy — this recurring use of the Italian word for friend.' Ballard grinned. 'Johnny Cassatta is no friend to anyone. He ran a number of rackets in Chicago, extremely lucrative ones. About two years ago he left.'

'You mean he had to disappear?'

Ballard shook his head. 'For no reason anybody knows, he simply quit. We heard he had gone to New York, but the report was unconfirmed. He could be in Los Angeles — or anywhere else. You have to realize that it meant little or nothing to us out here. Cassatta was just a name we knew something about, no more than that. None of us knew him personally. All our information was secondhand. It didn't matter so long as he didn't threaten us. But if he has moved out to California the position could be rather different.'

'And you don't even know what he looks like or what sort of man he is?'

'No, except that he's believed to have taken a legal degree.' Ballard chuckled sardonically. 'I don't imagine he's ever used it other than for essentially illegal purposes.'

There seemed to be little in it for me and I said: 'About Annette Falaise?'

He snapped on an ivory-lacquered annunciator box and spoke rapidly into it. He leaned back in his padded chair and observed: 'We'll know one way or the other within fifteen minutes, old chap — that is, if she's registered under her own name.' He passed a hand over his smooth dark hair and added slowly: 'You want to warn her that she is in danger . . . doesn't it occur to you that you could be in considerable danger yourself?'

'It has been suggested.'

'I mean right here in Las Vegas. If any of the men I've named are in The Organization they'll be on the lookout for you.' His eyes moved to Julie. 'Miss Arden may also be in a doubtful position.'

'Yeah,' I said. 'I think it would be better if we split up from now on.'

Julie leaned forward in a hide leather chair. 'I'm not being packed off home like a schoolgirl,' she said calmly. 'Besides, you don't even know for certain that these men are members of The Organization.'

'I applaud your courage while deploring your willingness to risk danger, Miss Arden,' murmured Ballard. 'If it'll help, I'll take steps with some associates to have all these men warned to get out of town.' He picked up a paper-knife and speared the tip in the desk blotter. 'You'll be safe here.'

The annunciator buzzed. He flipped a key and we listened to the incoming voice.

'Nobody named Annette Falaise has a hotel or rooming-house registration, Mr. Ballard.'

'You're absolutely sure?'

'Yeah, but . . . '

'What?'

'A woman who could be her bought a used car at a downtown lot and went north on Route Ninety-five.'

'Did she say where she was making for?'

'No, Mr. Ballard. But the sales clerk said she stopped at a liquor store nearby, so we checked there. She took on a quart of bonded whisky and bought a route map. The guy who sold it to her said she asked how long it'd take to make Reno.'

'Thanks, George,' said Ballard. 'You've done rather well.'

I said: 'Has she got friends there?'

Julie gestured helplessly. 'She never mentioned any, not to me.'

'And now I suppose you're also on the way, my dear Shand?' said Ballard.

'Yes, but not tonight. She'll have to put up somewhere. We can start about dawn. Suppose you stay on here until I catch up with her, Julie?'

'Suppose again.'

'I'll see that you're looked after better than a visiting movie queen, Miss Arden,' murmured Ballard.

She stood up, cool and defiant. 'I'm coming with you, Dale,' she said.

'All right. I'll just have to use my ingenuity to see that you keep out of the way if trouble starts again.'

Ballard gave us his strong, firm hand. 'I wish you both well,' he said. 'Meanwhile, be by guests at dinner. The place is all yours. By the way, just for the record,

Carelli isn't in town.'

'Why, should he be?'

'Not that I am aware of. I'm merely saying that he isn't.' Ballard thought for a moment and went on: 'I have a theory that, sooner or later, he'll go to New York.'

'You mean to confront Cassatta and gain control of The Organization?'

'In the light of what you heard him saying on the phone down in Mexico it seems a probability.'

'That assumes that The Organization was in being or mooted around the time Carelli went to the pen,' I reflected. 'It's tenable, though. On the other hand, Cassatta — if it was him and there seems no reason to think otherwise — was in California only a night or two ago.'

'That doesn't mean he is still there, old boy. I'd say he came out to set up the nucleus of an organization here — that and to get rid of Carelli.' Ballard smiled. 'A task in which he would seem to have failed with signal success.'

We ate T-bone steaks in Ballard's restaurant, wandered round the club, took a few turns on the handkerchief-sized dance floor and left. It was twenty minutes of eleven when we got back to the hotel.

A man was standing at the reception desk, saying something to the night clerk. He was a big man with a closely-cropped head which made his ears look more prominent. Especially the left one.

It was a cauliflower ear . . .

16

I went softly across the floor. The desk clerk was saying: ' . . . I'm sorry, but we don't show the hotel register to out-siders . . . '

The big man handed him a look like a silent snarl. His head craned slightly forward. 'Ten bucks,' he said gently. 'Or this.' His hand swept inside his jacket and came out with a .25 automatic. A handbag gun, but not necessarily ladylike.

The clerk's jaw dropped.

'Take your choice, bud,' whispered the big man.

I rammed my automatic in the small of his back. He went as stiff as a mainshaft. 'Lay your gun on the counter,' I said.

He put it there. He made no attempt to turn or even to speak. I stepped back and said: 'All right — turn.'

His hands were raised to shoulder level as he came round slowly. The face which stared at me looked as if it had been edited and re-edited in a couple of hundred stand-up-and-slug-it-out ring fights. Short of throwing acid or taking an ice-pick to it, there was nothing more you could do to his face. It was a face which had been hit by everything except the Empire State Building.

The eyes in the face were as hard as freezing water — and as blank.

'Dandy Jim Longman, I presume,' I said.

Expression flitted into his eyes. 'Who're you?' His voice was a harsh rustle of sound, like air squeezing through a leaking cylinder gasket.

Without looking at the desk clerk I told him to ring Ballard's number. The call went through. I said: 'Get Mr. Ballard to the phone and tell him Dandy Jim Longman is here and looking for trouble.'

'Ballard . . . ' Longman mouthed the word. 'If you're calling Ballard you must be in with his boys. I don't want no trouble. I'll go.'

'Sure. They'll escort you to the city limits, you and the rest of your mob.'

'I said I'll go . . . you don't have to

189

send for the trouble boys.' He was forcing himself to be conciliatory and not doing too well with it; two pinpoints of red flared high on his battered face.

The clerk moved. I glanced at him, an involuntary movement. Longman started a rush. I turned the gun and laid it on his left cheek. The skin cracked. He yelped, clawing at the counter, but I had the automatic back on him. 'Next time I'll fire it,' I said.

He swayed sideways against the desk. 'You got the drop on me now, fellow,' he breathed. 'But there'll be another time. I'll remember you . . . yeah, I'll remember you real well.'

A car stopped outside. Three men came in. They looked as primly respectable as a trio of tycoons. The middle one said: 'I guess you're Shand?'

I saw Dandy Jim Longman's eyes jump. He was getting a piece of information for free and without looking at the register, though I guessed Annette Falaise was the name he had been searching for. But one thing was clear — The Organization gang in Las Vegas had been told about me.

But all I said was: 'This is Dandy Jim Longman. Ballard wants him out of town.'

'He'll go — within the next ten minutes.' The speaker smiled bleakly. 'On your feet, lug. You just bought yourself a ticket to the point of no return.'

They took him away. Julie came up and said: 'Now what do we do?'

'How badly do you want to sleep, Julie?'

'Not badly — unless it's with you.' She smiled. 'You mean we had better leave?'

'I guess so. I don't mean we're in much danger now. At least, not immediately.'

'I don't quite follow that, Dale.'

'Well, the fellow they just took away won't be in any position to do anything and it'll be some time before the rest can, if they're not rounded up.'

'I thought Mr. Ballard was going to have them all warned.'

'Warned off and shown out — if they can all be located. They might not be.'

'I see. You think we ought to put as many miles as possible between us and them?'

'It's a sensible idea, Julie. Remember — they don't yet know we're here and they're unlikely, even when they find out, to know which direction we take.'

'I'll get my things,' she said.

An hour later we were beyond Indian Springs going north on Route Ninety-five toward the eastern edge of Death Valley. It was a fine, clear night with not much traffic. I put the car heater on and Julie snuggled against me. 'How far are we driving?' she murmured.

'We'll make Beatty — that's approximately a hundred and twenty miles from Vegas. We can doze in the car for an hour and then drive on. There's a road west across Death Valley to Lone Pine just below the High Sierras. From there we can pick up the U.S. thru route which goes north all the way to Reno.'

'Whatever you say, Dale,' she said sleepily.

Time passed. The miles swept behind us. The motor was humming, a continuous tight drone. The crisp night air seemed to suit it — or is that a motoring fallacy? The experts say so, but I'm not a great man for experts; when I was a newspaper reporter I heard too many of them being either wrong or limited in their judgments.

The steady hum induced thought — and what I was thinking about was something more than the immediate aim of warning Annette Falaise. The wider implications of what I had got myself into were clear enough and I ought to have thought about them before, but too much had been happening. Now, on the long night drive north, they crowded in on me. If they meant anything they implied a new network of crime — a cartel of ruthless and resourceful men establishing its locals, appointing regional henchmen ready for a major take-over, muscling-in on a hundred sources of easy money. It seemed beyond credibility that the law could be in total ignorance; somewhere along the line information always leaks. But in this formative stage the information could be vague and inconclusive. The picture shaping in my mind was of a disciplined and highly-organized group whose real purpose might not become apparent until a *fait accompli* had been achieved. And behind it all the executive genius of a man I had never seen, though I had heard his voice — the man whose sole betraying idiosyncracy was a sardonic addiction to the use of the word *amico*. But of one thing I was certain . . . I would know the voice again.

As if she were keeping pace with what I was thinking, Julie suddenly said: 'That man whose voice you heard in the house they took you to . . . '

'Yes?'

'You weren't intended to leave with the knowledge of that voice, Dale. They'll hunt you down, no matter where you go.'

'They'll try. Right now they don't have any idea where I am. If I thought otherwise I'd put you down by the roadside, for your own safety.'

'I told you I'm in this with you, Dale. I won't go.'

'I'll make you, if I have to and . . . '

Something darted into the road and turned. I flicked the spotlight on. The beam lit up two staring, luminous eyes like golden orbs. Then they were gone.

'What was that?' exclaimed Julie.

'A polecat.' I lit two cigarettes and passed one to her. 'When we catch-up with Annette I'm going right back to Los Angeles and turn over what information I have to Logan and the District Attorney.'

'I hope they won't be too mad at you.'

'They know I didn't kill that guy in the hotel,' I said. 'Hammer virtually said as much over the phone. Not that I expect to get a civic welcome.' A thought occurred to me and I went on: 'We haven't been listening to the radio, and that's a mistake.'

She switched it on, roving from one station to another. Pop music, a soap opera, a Western, a situation comedy full of over-slick characterization and gagbook jokes, a newscast. But nothing about the law wanting to trace the whereabouts of Dale Shand, private investigator. Maybe there had been, though, and we had missed it.

More miles. I figured we were now less than fifteen due south of Beatty. Lights blazed behind us, swelling in volume.

Julie said: 'We're doing seventy. Who-ever's behind us must be really travelling.'

I eased my foot off the pedal and pulled over to give him all the room he wanted. It was a fast car all right, a Sting Ray. It surged past with a gutty throb from the chromed twin exhausts. I caught a glimpse of a couple of hard white faces staring straight ahead with go-to-hell expressions.

They didn't mean anything to me.

17

It was nearing two in the morning when we drove into the outskirts of Beatty. The road curled between tree-lined slopes. Round one of the bends and midway up the slope a motel spelled its name in a winking three-colour sequence.

'We're going to get some sleep,' I said. 'About four hours of it.'

'I'm willing to carry on, Dale.'

'No, we ought to have some rest. We won't lose anything — Annette will have to stop somewhere.'

'I'm beginning to wonder if we'll ever find her.'

'We'll do it, Julie. Every river has to wind to the sea, as they say.'

I drove up the gravelled approach and on to the forecourt. The office was open and a man was sitting behind the counter next to a small telephone switchboard. He looked up as we came in. He was small and neat with a smooth boyish face, though he wasn't a boy any more.

'You want a room?' he asked. His voice was slightly muffled, as if he had sinus trouble.

'If you have one, yes.'

'There's five vacant, we're not busy just now.' He pushed the register across the counter and went on: 'Double room with shower, twenty dollars. You can back your car up to the entrance and take your things out.'

'We'll do that.'

'You have to pay in advance.'

'Sure.'

'What time d'you want calling?'

'Six-thirty.'

'You'll not be getting much sleep,' he said. 'You must be in a hurry.'

'It's the end of our vacation and we've still a long drive home.'

He put an unlit cigarette in his mouth, jiggled it from one side to the other and said: 'You'd better have the keys.' As he spoke he looked through the open door. The car was right outside. A sudden odd look came into his eyes. Then he yawned, stretched himself and stood up. 'I guess you're tired,' he said. 'I'll get your cases out for you.'

'That's nice of you,' I said.

He strolled through the doorway with his hands in his pants pockets and the cigarette still unlit.

Julie looked at me. 'I don't like him,' she said.

I didn't answer. I was looking through the open door. He was standing behind the car. His lips moved as if he were repeating something to himself in order to memorize it. He lit the cigarette, dropped the match and started getting the cases out. When he came back he glanced down at the register. I had written *John and Mary Warren* in it.

'I'll see if I can fix some coffee,' he said carelessly. 'The kitchen staff are off duty, but I'll fix it for you myself. Room Nineteen, I think you'll like it there.'

I backed the car up, got out and walked close enough to the office to see without being seen. He was telephoning, just like the man in the petrol station had done. I couldn't hear what he was saying. He could have been calling his girl friend, but

I didn't think so. He put the receiver down and disappeared through a rear door. The twenty dollars I had paid him was still lying on the counter. I walked in and picked it up.

When I got back Julie was standing by the car. 'We'll not be stopping here after all,' I said. 'I think he's had a police message to look out for us.'

I dumped the cases in the back of the car. He must have heard the motor start up because he came dashing out of his little office. We went down the approach and turned on to the road. From where he stood he could see the direction we were taking — due north on Route Ninety-five with fifty miles to go to the next town, which was Goldfield.

'If he's called the police they'll follow us,' said Julie.

'Yeah — and soon. He saw the way we went. He'll go back and tell them.'

I drove through the sleeping town and beyond. The road speared into the far distance, empty. Julie turned in her seat. 'Nothing yet . . . '

'They're not so fast as all that,' I

grinned. 'We've time enough.'

'You mean time to out-distance them?'

'No. They'll catch-up with us all right — if we give them the chance. That's what we're not going to do.' I drove fifteen miles almost flat out, then turned the car round and doubled back on our tracks.

'They'll see us as they pass,' Julie said.

'They won't,' I answered. I kept on driving, but not for long. After another mile the road went into a sweeping right-hand curve. I backed the car completely off the roadway, rumbling up a wooded slope and into a small clearing and cut all the lights.

A light wind rose, soughing through the trees. A small animal scurried away in the darkness, snapping a twig. It sounded like the crack of doom. Then silence. Minutes passed and nothing happened. Julie got a cigarette out and a lighter. I closed a hand over it.

'I'm sorry,' she whispered. 'The light . . . I didn't think.'

'They might see it, Julie.'

'If they come.'

'They'll come.'

She made a small shiver. I said: 'Are you cold?'

'No, frightened. I don't know why.'

'It's the waiting.'

Then, abruptly, there was no more waiting. Headlights blazed up the straight section beyond the big sweeping bend. Less than half a minute later a police car roared past at an easy ninety and was gone.

I grinned. 'You can light that cigarette now,' I said.

'I need it. I'll give you one.'

'All right.' I edged the car down on to the road and drove fast but not over-fast toward Beatty — but not all the way. A paved road thrust westwards from the thru route and we took it.

Half an hour later we were out of Nevada territory. We were in Death Valley.

18

Once they called it the place of desolation and tragedy — a vast submerged floor of scorched and parched earth and sparse plant life struggling desperately for survival. That was before Death Valley became a national monument and an 'in' resort for people who can pay for a winter vacation as well as a summer one. At that time of the year the days here are still warm and sunny, the nights cool and clear and invigorating.

It was the last day of September when we saw it for the first time, or as much of it as you can see under a half moon. Tomorrow, if we had the time, we could look down on Bad Water, two hundred and eighty feet below sea level, and up at distant Mount Whitney rearing its craggy bulk nearly fifteen thousand feet skywards . . . the lowest and highest points in the United States.

Now, flowing and spreading all around

us, there was nothing but the endless barren land touched by the pale lunar radiance, like the endless landscape of a lost world.

'It's eerie here at night,' said Julie.

'Frightened, just a little?'

'No, not really. Besides, in some way it's strangely beautiful.'

'You're beautiful, Julie.'

She smiled. 'But not strange, not any more.'

'You've never seemed like a stranger to me, not even when I first saw you,' I said.

'Truly?'

'Truly.'

'What did you think when we first met?'

'Now you're asking the kind of question women always ask.'

'Why not? After all, I am a woman. What did you think?'

'That you were beautiful and that I liked you immediately.'

'But you didn't expect to make love to me?'

'No, I didn't expect that.'

'Did you want to?'

'Most men have that unbidden thought when they meet a pretty girl,' I said. 'But, no, I had no notion of doing it, or even attempting it.'

'And even if you had you couldn't have imagined the setting . . . the sand almost like a hot plate under us.'

'I guess we didn't notice it until later, did we?'

'No, which must prove something.'

'What?'

'Oh, get along with you,' she said. She peered ahead. 'We still seem to be in the middle of nowhere.'

'Well, I never heard of a lot of towns in Death Valley. So far as I know, there's nothing except a vacation hotel or two and some dude ranches.'

'Dude Shand, the gun-toting sleuth?' she mocked.

'It's a nine-shot Colt automatic.'

'Too modern.'

'Yes, I should be wearing a Frontier Colt with an eight-inch barrel and a filed-down sight, like Zach Gunnery has.'

'Now who on earth is that?'

'A sheriff I got friendly with on a case

up in Long Island.'

'And he was wearing a gun like that? I thought they were museum-pieces.'

'Well, they're still issued to some Western peace officers. It was odd finding a sheriff on Long Island with one, though.'

'Was he as nice as Sheriff Tom Peel?'

'As a matter of fact, there was a similarity between them. Not so much in physical appearance, but in their personalities. I'd say that if they met they'd get along fine together.'

'You seemed to get along fine with Tom Peel.'

'Yes.'

'And with this other one on Long Island, too?'

'I guess I did.'

'And yet you're a city dweller.'

'By an accident of circumstance. I told Tom Peel about that. I grew up in a small community in the Mid-West . . . ' I grinned. 'I told you about that, too, didn't I?'

'Yes. Anyway, you seem to meet only the nicest sheriffs.'

'Well, let's keep our fingers crossed we don't run into any of the other kind.'

'We don't seem likely to meet anybody at all in this emptiness,' answered Julie.

'Perhaps it's as well.'

'Why — do you mean we could run into trouble?'

'I don't think so, not immediately, though you never can tell. But the fewer people we meet just now the better. Not that the Nevada law know we're here.'

'Suppose they find out?'

'How are they going to do that? Nobody saw us leave the thru route for Death Valley. In fact, after we headed back toward Beatty we saw nothing of traffic. That police car's probably still going north looking for us. By the time we get through this place they could be heading up into the Shoshone Mountains.'

Julie giggled. 'Just to think of those poor men losing their beauty sleep resolutely driving in the wrong direction.'

'Why not? We're losing ours.'

'But when they don't catch-up with us they'll do something, won't they?'

'Such as what? They'll figure we made a detour and lost them, that's all. By that time it won't matter — at least, not to us.'

An hour later the road joined Route 190. We could either press straight on or bear left down to Furnace Creek. I kept straight on. Dawn was sweeping the velvet dark from the sky, adding flecks of amber and old gold to the spreading blue, when we finally drove out of Death Valley and took the winding road north. We ate ham and eggs at a wayside café on the outskirts of Lone Pine and drove on again.

A hundred miles later we were running into Crestview, almost within sight of the Yosemite National Park. It was high noon after a night with virtually no sleep and too much driving, much too much driving. Julie took her compact out and touched-up her face. It still looked young and fresh. She held the mirror out and I looked at mine. It needed a shave and the eyes needed a couple of bamboo poles to prop them up.

'I'm too old for you, Julie,' I said.

'Now what's the matter with you?' she demanded.

'Nothing, except that I've just seen my reflection in the mirror. It wrecked the image I had formed of myself as a swashbuckling young cavalier jousting with dastardly villains and riding off with fair maidens.'

'You're not doing badly in either of those departments . . . '

'Just the same, you ought to have somebody younger. Not a guy with an unshaven, ravaged face and bleary eyes.'

'It's a beautiful face and I love it, shaven or unshaven, clear-eyed or bleary-eyed.'

'We need some more gas,' I said.

'Do we?'

'Yeah. Preferably a place where we can eat and washup as well.'

'I can see a place from here, down the road. It might do.'

'We'll try it, anyway.' I drove there. It was a biggish service station with a restaurant and rest-rooms. Girls in Western clothes were manning the pumps.

They looked young, cool and well-adjusted. Well, they weren't thirty-nine years old and they hadn't been driving all night with an odd snatch or two of sleep.

One of them drifted up with a wide, friendly smile, looking like Doris Day in full Technicolor. 'How many, sir?'

'It's a twelve-gallon tank, put ten in,' I told her.

'Sure — that way you don't have to drive with the smell of gasolene.' She unhooked the hose and I reached for my billfold.

Julie turned toward me, one hand on my arm. 'The used car Annette bought in Las Vegas — it was a 1963 powder blue Chevrolet with a crimson roof, wasn't it?'

'Yes — why?'

'Look over there, Dale — in the parking bay behind the other line of pumps.'

I looked. The description fitted all right. I walked over to it. The car was locked, but there was a small cambric handkerchief on the bench seat close to the driving position.

The handkerchief was lying flat. Embroidered in one corner of it were the initials *A.F.*

It looked as if the chase was over.

19

I went back. The girl cowboy took my money and brought some change. I pocketed part of it and said: 'There's a pale blue Chevvy in the bay. The owner is a friend of ours. Is she around?'

The girl smiled. 'I couldn't say, sir. She might be in the restaurant or the powder room. You could ask.'

'I'll do it,' Julie said. She got out of the car and went into the main building. I sat there playing offbeats on the steering wheel and resisting a desire to smoke made the more insistent by the notice forbidding it on the forecourt.

Then Julie was back. 'They say Annette has gone on a bus trip to the Yosemite National Park. Well, of course they didn't actually say Annette. They said the owner of the car and I described her and they said it was her.'

I turned to the girl in the ranch clothes. 'Can I leave my car?'

'Certainly — but not right where it is. Put it in one of the bays, sir.'

I drove the car where she showed me and walked across to the restaurant with Julie. She said: 'You don't seem terribly excited.'

'I thought I would be when we finally caught-up with her, but somehow I'm not. It's the climax to everything we've been doing, and yet it seems like an anti-climax. Did you find out what time the bus gets back, by the way?'

'Yes. Not for another three hours.'

I grunted. 'Why on earth is she taking side trips to peer at the scenery?'

'Well, for goodness sake, why shouldn't she?'

'No reason, I suppose, but . . . '

'She probably thinks she's safe now and fancied an outing. The Yosemite's worth a trip, I imagine. What are we going to do — wait for her?'

'Well, we could do with some food and a rest.'

'I wouldn't mind seeing the Yosemite while we're here, Dale.'

'We'll have a drink while we

decide what to do.'

'A nice long cool drink with lots of ice-cream and fruit for me.'

'I'll have a nice long cool drink with lots of Scotch.'

'I thought perhaps you might,' Julie answered.

They had a bar down one side of the restaurant and I was about to order when I glanced through the wide rear window. Beyond it was another parking lot and one of the cars was a crimson Sting Ray.

The bartender was saying something, but it was a distant jumble of words. I pulled myself together and ordered. Julie pulled at my sleeve and said: 'Dale — what's wrong?'

'Take a hard look through the rear window,' I said.

'Why, what is it?'

'There's a car out there, a crimson convertible. Just take a look at it and come back.'

She stared at me, then walked across the floor. When she returned her face was animated. 'It's the Sting Ray that passed

214

us on the way to Lone Pine — I'm sure of it.'

'How sure? There's more than one of that model around.'

'Yes, but when it passed us I noticed that the boot had a dinge in it, on the right-hand side, as if it had been backed up against something or bumped by another car.'

I breathed harshly down my nose, not saying anything.

'You didn't see the dinge?' asked Julie.

'No, I was preoccupied looking at the two guys in the car.'

'Well, it's the same one, Dale.'

'And they're not here.' I stared round in case I had missed them, but I hadn't. Then I said: 'Hell, we're letting ourselves get rattled. Why shouldn't they be here? We're here — and lots of others.' Just the same, I felt uneasy.

The bartender served another customer. When he was through I leaned over and said: 'There's a red Sting Ray parked on the rear lot. It belongs to a couple of friends. Do you happen to know if they're around?'

He threw a fast glance towards the window, turned back and said conversationally: 'Yeah, know who you mean. Two fellows, very pale in the face like they haven't been out here long. They went on the trip to the Yosemite, sort of.'

'How do you mean, they sort of went on it?'

'Well, they didn't join the bus party on account of the bus had already gone. They left their car here for some servicing and hired a Land Rover, one of them English heaps. We got several here. Sometimes folks prefer to use them on trips. Useful in some circumstances, like if they want to leave the road and go over any rough ground.'

'I see.' The drink I had bought was right in front of me, but I didn't any longer want a drink. I had something else on my mind now. 'Did they go immediately after the bus left?'

'Not at once — soon after, though.'

I made a laugh full of spurious affability. 'Well, what do you know? It seems to be our day for catching-up with old friends. Another one actually went on

216

the bus trip. A lady friend.'

'She did?' He was politely uninterested.

'That's right.' I described Annette to him, purely on the off-chance that he might have seen her.

He nodded. 'Well, it cert'nly is your day. What's more, the two guys you're talking about were interested in her.'

'Oh?'

'Yeah, and that's kind of funny because she didn't seem to know them. She was in here and walked out right past them as they came in.'

'And they didn't speak to her?'

'Nope, they just walked on up to this bar. But I heard one of them saying something about her being the one. They were having a drink and I just happened to hear what they said.'

'Maybe they mistook her for somebody else,' I said.

The bartender shook his head. 'The fellow said it looked like her and must be on account of it was the car all right. I didn't hear any more.' He eyed me curiously.

'I expect they just thought they knew

her,' I said carelessly. 'They could have been misled by the make of car.'

'There's sump'n odd about it, though,' he mused. He leaned both elbows on the bar. 'I mean them saying that and then you asking questions.'

'It's probably nothing,' I said. 'Especially as they didn't speak to her.'

'Well, I guess that's true. They just had a couple of drinks and went off. By that time the lady had left with the bus party. I seen the two fellows drive away in the Land Rover — that's how I know they had it.'

I thought for a moment, then said: 'Is there another Land Rover available?'

'Could be — you inquire over there.' He pointed at a door.

'Thanks.' I palmed him a dollar and we left before he could ask any more questions. He had the look of a man well loaded with questions.

The office was behind a screen door. I pushed it open and went in. The place was empty. 'We can't wait,' I said. 'We'll use our own car.'

'Do you really think these two men

have gone after her?' Julie asked.

'They must have.'

'But how would they know her car?'

'Look, Ballard's men found out that she'd bought one. What Ballard can do The Organization can do, too.'

'I thought Ballard was going to warn them off?'

'Maybe he didn't locate them all. One or more of them found out that she'd bought a car and was going this way. They must have followed — after all, we did. Besides, they'd have a description of her. It's my guess that they identified her in a general way — and the car clinched it.'

'Yes . . . yes, you must be right.'

We were back in our own car now and I was driving off. 'If you look at the position in the light of these two factors, it isn't a coincidence,' I went on. 'As to our getting wise to them, even that isn't entirely chance. We both recognized the convertible. The piece of luck we had was that bartender remembering a few facts.'

'He was starting to get curious, wasn't he?'

'Very.' I dipped the car down into the

valley. Massed granite domes rose from the sides of the deep green floor, interlaced with stupendous cataracts and long slim waterfalls feathery as swansdown. Vacation trippers strolled on the grass or stood below tall, elegant trees with unslung cameras. A girl in sky-blue jeans and a white nylon shirt went past in a British sports car, going back toward Crestview. A dark-haired boy with a freckled face and the physique of a Greek god wolf-whistled as she went by, then resumed walking. Two lovers sauntered with their arms round each other, not seeing anything except themselves; they could have been no less happy strolling through the meanest quarter of The Bowery.

Suddenly, Julie said: 'Down there . . . look!'

I braked and stared. Two men were standing close to a line of six trees thrusting their slim trunks upwards against the backdrop of the Yosemite Falls. They were the two I had seen in the Sting Ray. There was no sign of the Land Rover they had hired; they must have left it and gone ahead on foot.

'What do we do now?' asked Julie in a low voice.

'Get closer,' I answered.

We walked down the gentle slope to where they were standing. The man I had seen driving glanced casually around. His pale, sharp face gave no sign of recognition. He turned back to the other man and said: 'She's not around here, Al. We'd better go back to the Land Rover and try some place else.'

'The trippers left the bus over there, Ugo,' his companion said. He jerked his head at an angle.

'Sure, but they went off on foot. She can't have got far.' Ugo lit a cigarette and breathed twin streams of smoke down his nostrils. 'The quicker we do this the better . . . we got to make Virginia City sometime today . . . '

'Yeah, we got a date with O'Hara!' The man called Al made a rustle of sound in his throat. It could have been intended as a laugh.

They drifted away. I went on standing there, looking up at the magnificent splendour of the Falls without really seeing it.

I heard Julie say: 'If we locate the bus we might find out if Annette's still with the party and where they've gone.'

I didn't answer. I was still staring up at the Falls and this time I saw them. I also saw something else — a figure almost on the summit. Someone who wanted to get the perfect panoramic view. It was impossible to identify the figure with any certainty at this distance, but it looked like the figure of a woman.

'You weren't listening, Dale,' said Julie.

I cupped her left elbow and said: 'There's someone up on the summit, a woman.'

'Goodness . . . it could be Annette.'

'It could be anybody.'

'Well, if we get closer we'll find out.'

I started to say something, but stopped. In the distance, beyond the trees, two figures appeared, climbing. One of them was some way in front of the other. They were the men from the Sting Ray.

A conducted group of sightseers came up, chattering. I heard the guide say:

'That's one of our party up there . . . she said she was going up to the top.'

Julie turned to him and said: 'Is she a Miss Falaise?'

'That's her name, miss. But you ain't with the bus party.'

I said: 'No, but we'd like to join her. Do you happen to know a short cut to the summit?'

'Why, yeah. There's a direct route.' He told us how to find it. 'It's just a bridle path, but it's quicker than any other way. It starts from behind those trees — over there on your right.'

The path was steep and narrow, but it was direct, as he had said. I got to the top first and started through some trees toward the sheer drop of the Falls.

Then, suddenly, I saw her. She was standing alone, a motionless figure in a white wool sweater and a pleated tan skirt, looking down at the descending water.

'Annette!' I called.

She didn't turn. The thunder of the Falls had blotted out my voice. I went forward and had opened my mouth to yell when the man called Ugo came from another cluster of trees and coarse brushwood on the other side of her. He was moving without hurry, like a hunter stalking prey.

I emerged from the cover of the last trees and used all the power in my lungs.

'Annette — look out. Run!'

She heard me. But so did Ugo. He jumped at her as she wheeled and saw him. Her mouth opened in an unheard cry . . . then she almost hurled herself sideways out of his path.

He landed on the uneven ground where she had been standing. Loose stones slithered under his feet. His body craned forward, both hands clawing at the air. For a split second he seemed about to regain his balance . . . then his left foot slipped and he plunged headlong over the sheer drop of the Falls.

A high thin scream rose above the tumult of the water, then died in it.

20

I grabbed her as she swayed, her body shaking against mine. Far below at the base of the Falls micro-men moved, tiny figures running, looking for Ugo.

'Dale . . . Oh, Dale . . . ' She clung almost violently to me, half-sobbing.

'It's all right, you're safe,' I said.

I steered her away from the summit, toward the trees. She was hanging on to me, sideways, both hands clasped round my neck. Hands like ice.

'That man . . . what was he trying to do to me?' She didn't wait for an answer, but rushed on. 'I . . . I thought he meant to kill me . . . '

'No, it wasn't that, Annette. He was going to recapture you — kidnap you, the second time round. There were two of them.' As I spoke I managed to look back. There was no sign of the other man. He must have seen what had happened, though. I judged he would be on his way back to Crestview.

Julie came out of the fringe of trees. She put an arm round Annette, helping her down the bridle path. The trembling began to fade and Annette said wonderingly: 'Julie . . . what are you doing here . . . how . . . '

'It's a long story, we'll tell you when you're feeling better, honey.'

'I've had such a dreadful, dreadful time . . . '

'It's all over now,' I said gently.

We were close to the bottom of the bridle path when she said: 'I'm feeling a little better. How did you find me?'

Julie smiled. 'You can thank Dale for it all — he's the most doggedly persistent man I ever met.'

'I knew he was nice,' Annette said. 'I knew it when we met by chance in that bar. But I never imagined I'd ever see him again.'

I grinned. 'We've been on your trail ever since you left Los Angeles. Incidentally, why did you?'

She bit down on her lip. 'I was upset seeing Dino. Then I got to thinking about him . . . I was frightened that he'd somehow find me, perhaps run into me on the street . . . I . . . I didn't want to see him again . . . '

'So you ran away?'

'Yes. Well, it seemed the only thing to do.'

'It wasn't Dino you needed to be frightened about,' I said grimly. 'The men who kidnapped you — didn't they tell you?'

'Tell me what?' She stared uncomprehendingly.

'Just after you left a man came down into the bar. He was looking for your ex-husband — with a gun.'

She shivered again.

'A criminal syndicate calling itself The Organization sent this man to kill Dino. But Carelli was faster — he shot the killer straight between the eyes.'

For a long moment she said nothing. Then she whispered: 'But what has this to do with me . . . why should these dreadful men kidnap me?'

'The Organization think you can finger Carelli for them,' I said. I told her why, adding: 'Julie figured you had gone south of the border, so we started after you. Then a lot of other things began happening, one after the other.' I said what they were.

She looked up at me. 'But I know nothing . . . nothing of Dino's whereabouts or anything else.'

'These men who kidnapped you don't believe that, Annette. That explains everything that's been going on.'

'Well, it's absurd,' she cried. 'I couldn't tell them a thing, so what could they possibly do?'

I hesitated, but it was better that she should know. I said levelly: 'They would try to force something out of you . . . they're rather adept at it.'

A small stricken cry burst from her. 'Oh, God . . . you mean they'd torture me?'

'Yes. It would be worse because you're literally unable to tell them a thing. Don't worry — they'll not get another chance.'

We came off the bridle path and started through the trees towards the grass. The guide I had seen previously showed up and gasped: 'You all right, Miss Falaise?'

'Yes,' she said, 'I'm all right now.'

'Some guy jumped at you up there,' he said. 'We could see it from down below. You turned just in time. I guess this gentleman must've shouted a warning?'

She nodded and the guide went on: 'That guy who tried to attack you . . . I reckon he's paid for it. They've just dragged his body out of the water. We'd better put you in the bus and get you back to Crestview.'

'She can come in our car,' I said.

He seemed uncertain and Annette said: 'It's all right. They're both very dear friends of mine. In fact, they were looking for me.'

'Yeah, I remember he said something about that,' the guide answered. 'If you want a doctor we can fix that.'

'It's kind of you, but I'm going to be all right,' she replied.

We were half-way back to Crestview when she spoke again. 'I feel so safe and happy now,' she said.

I answered without turning: 'The safest place for you from now on is Los Angeles

— with full police protection.'

'You mean you're taking me back — going with me?'

I nodded. 'I've done what I wanted to do — located you, Annette. I promised the captain of detectives that I'd come back then. We'll send our car on a freight train and get a flight out of Reno tomorrow. You'll probably have to make a statement to the authorities here first.'

'Whatever you say, Dale.' She smiled tremulously. 'For the first time in what seems like a nightmare eternity I feel safe. I think I've had more than enough adventure to last me the rest of my life.' She closed her hand on mine for a brief moment.

'I guess you could use a drink,' I said.

She shook her head. 'No. I bought some liquor in Vegas, but I never touched it. I think something's happened to me. I don't want the stuff any more.'

'I'm glad.'

She fell silent, sitting between Julie and myself on the wide bench seat of the car. Then, slowly, she resumed: 'I'd got to the stage when I was only living for the next drink. I kept thinking about it, knowing I was becoming an alcoholic — or was already one. But I felt so desperately ill and I had to have more drinks to get rid of the feeling, knowing that by morning I'd be ill again, and worse. I used to hide the liquor behind curtains, under the sink, anywhere so that visitors wouldn't see it . . . even so that I didn't see it myself. The capacity an alcoholic has for self-deception and lying is limitless . . . '

Julie looked troubled, but neither of us spoke.

Annette went on, still in the same slow tone: 'When I left Vegas I realized I would have to stay sober if I hoped to drive fast and safely. Then I began to feel different . . . better. It suddenly came to me that if I could do without the stuff for a day perhaps I could do without it altogether. Besides, I'd done a lot of unaccustomed thinking while I was a prisoner. I guess I'd had a chance given me to look at my life . . . and what I saw was pretty lousy. I can't explain it really . . . all I know is that I didn't any longer want a drink.'

'Have you quit thinking about it?'

'Yes — that, too. It doesn't seem to matter any more. I believe I'm off the hook.'

I grinned faintly. 'If you ever feel that you're in danger of weakening, you'd better get yourself kidnapped again,' I said.

'Not that! Once and for all time is enough.'

We were back in Crestview. From the restaurant window I could still see the crimson Sting Ray. There was nobody in it. Maybe Al hadn't got back yet. I'd be looking out for him. In the meantime, I ordered coffee and said: 'We'd better drive you to Reno.'

'Yes.'

'What will you do about the car you bought?'

'I don't know. It doesn't matter.'

'They buy cars here,' I said. 'I saw a notice. If you like, I'll see what they offer.'

'Whatever it is, take it, Dale.'

I nodded. We finished the coffee. I went across the floor to one of the offices. Through the main glass doors of the restaurant I saw a Land Rover rumble on to the forecourt. The man who answered to the name of Al climbed out.

I went back to the table and said: 'The fellow who was with Ugo, he's just shown.'

Annette shivered.

'You come with me while I see about selling your car,' I said. 'Julie will keep her eye on him. He doesn't know her and she can watch with impunity, as it were.'

Julie laughed. 'It'll be better if I watch with unerring accuracy,' she said.

'If you take a casual stroll to the forecourt you'll have him in view.'

'Suppose he just gets in the car and goes?'

I shrugged. 'I guess we can't do a thing to stop him. He wasn't with the other guy at the time and we can't prove anything. Just the same, I'd like . . . '

'You'd like what?'

'I'd like to think I could put him in custody, that's what. But if we call up some law we'll get bogged down in a mass of procedural boondoggling — and at the end of it we still won't be able to prove a thing.'

'Well, I'll keep an eye on him in case he shows signs of moving toward you and Annette.'

'He hasn't seen her, and even if he did he'll be too smart to try anything as long as she's with me.'

Julie started for the main entrance. She turned once and called softly: 'He's still out there on the forecourt, taking something out of the Land Rover.'

I nodded and walked with Annette Falaise into the office with an *Auto Sales* legend on the door. Ten minutes later we had sold her car. The book price wasn't exciting, but the heap was five years old. Annette signed a receipt, put the money in her handbag and we went back into the restaurant. Julie wasn't at the entrance. She wasn't out on the forecourt, either. Neither was Al. Maybe he had gone to get the Sting Ray and she had followed him. I walked round the rear and looked. The red car wasn't there. Nor was Julie.

Annette came alongside. 'Where can she have gone?' she said.

'I don't know,' I answered. We waited minutes, then went into the restaurant again. I had a sudden growing sensation of unease.

'She could have gone into the powder room,' Annette suggested. 'I'll go and look.'

She went away and I stood there thinking. Something had occurred to me, something I should have calculated on — the possibility that he had glanced in the restaurant and seen me talking with Julie and Annette. Sweat began crawling down my spine and it was zero cold.

Annette came out of the powder room shaking her head. I grabbed her arm and went round the back again. One of the girl attendants looked at us inquiringly.

Harshly, I said: 'There was a crimson convertible out here, a Sting Ray.'

'Yes, sir. I filled the tank . . . ' She was staring hard at my face. It must have been a mask of anxiety.

'Did you see it when it was driven off?'

'Yes, it was ten or more minutes ago.'

'Who was in it?'

She hesitated and I said urgently: 'For God's sake, it's important — *who was in it?*'

'A man was driving,' she answered, 'but there was a girl with him, a girl with coppery hair.' She eyed me curiously and went on: 'As a matter of fact, she looked like she didn't want to be in the car with him and I figured they must have had a fuss, but he sort of pushed her in with his left hand . . . '

'With his right hand in his jacket pocket,' I said thickly.

'Why, that's right, and . . . '

But I was already running back to the car with Annette Falaise.

21

We were through Lee Vining and going north to Bridgeport before Annette spoke. She had sat without movement, staring through the window, as the road came towards us.

'It's all my fault,' she said. 'It's all . . . ' Her voice was lost in the thunder of a truck going the other way. Then it came back, dully, as if she were speaking to herself. 'They've got Julie and but for me it would never have happened and . . . '

'Shut up!' I snarled the words at her. Tears ran down her face and her mouth trembled. 'I'm sorry,' I said. 'I didn't even mean it. My nerves are cut in strips.'

She dabbed at her eyes with a small cambric handkerchief like the one I had seen in her car. 'It's all right, Dale . . . you must be half crazy with desperation.'

'Yes.' I took the car through the town and on toward the double bend before Sonora Junction. 'Only it's not your fault,

Annette. If it's anybody's it's mine. If I hadn't left Julie alone everything would have been all right.'

She moved restlessly and said: 'But . . . why did he do it? It's me these men think they want. Julie knows nothing about Dino . . . why in heavens' name did he do it?'

'The man who forced her into his car must have seen me when I warned you at the Falls,' I said savagely. 'It's my guess that he's realized who I am — and taken Julie as a reprisal.'

She seemed to shrink back in her seat. 'Oh, God . . . what will . . . ' Her voiced faded into nothingness.

'I don't think they'll hurt her — not yet,' I said. 'This is almost certainly more than a reprisal. They'll hold her as a hostage.'

'I don't understand,' Annette whispered.

'They want you and they want me. One or both of us will be the price of Julie's freedom.'

She stared bewilderedly. 'But how on earth are they going to contact you?'

'They'll find a way.'

'How?'

'A television or radio newscast, an item in the newspapers, even an ultimatum through the police . . . whatever it is they need they'll find a way.'

'They might even find *you*, Dale,' she said in a low voice.

'It's a possibility, yes . . . unless we can catch-up with the kidnapper first.'

'You mean before he can get in touch with the others?'

I nodded. 'We'll hear nothing until they're ready, Annette. That may be hours, maybe days. But remember . . . he's got no more than somewhere between ten and fifteen minutes start on us.' I felt my mouth twist on itself. 'In the car he's driving that's more than plenty, but we have one advantage — I know where he's going.'

'What!'

'Before we spotted you at the head of the Yosemite Falls we heard them talking. They said they were making for Virginia City.'

Her eyes widened. 'Why would they go

there?' she asked.

'They said something about keeping an appointment with a man named O'Hara . . . ' Suddenly, I felt her body stiffen beside me. 'That name,' I said, 'it means something to you, doesn't it?'

'Yes, I think so.'

'What?'

'I haven't heard the name in ages — but Dino knew a man named O'Hara. He was involved in some rackets in Reno. In fact, he was a close associate if not a friend of Dino's.'

'You mean he's a hot shot?'

'I don't know, not to be sure, but I think he was in the rackets.' She smiled sadly. 'If he was with Dino he likely would be.'

'It's a tenable proposition,' I answered dryly.

'But it doesn't get us anywhere, does it?' she asked.

'It could do. If Dino is planning to take over control of this new syndicate he would look for old friends, men he could count on. Maybe O'Hara is one of them.'

'I suppose so. I know Dino thought a lot of O'Hara.'

'What's he like?'

'I never met him. I only heard Dino speak of him. Once, though, he called Dino on long-distance and they were talking for an hour and a half, but I never actually saw him.'

I drove on, thinking. Then I said slowly: 'If this man O'Hara is in Virginia City maybe Dino is going there — if he isn't there already. It could be that the man who snatched Julie will have a surprise waiting for him, unless . . . '

'Unless what?' she asked uncertainly.

'Well, The Organization could be using it as a meeting-place. Nobody would think of an executive session of crime taking place in Virginia City.'

She stretched out a hand to touch me. 'You can't take them all on single-handed,' she said.

'Maybe they're not meeting there. Come to think of it, these two men wouldn't have talked about seeing O'Hara if The Organization was already in occupation. But, in any event, what choice do I have? There's no time to contact the law — and what sort of reception would I get if I did?'

'The police would have to listen, have to help you . . . they'd have to do *something* . . . '

'Like what? The chances are they've had a teletype message about me and the first thing I'd know they'd be sending me back to L.A. under escort.'

'It's hopeless, isn't it?'

'Nothing is hopeless, Annette. Somehow I have to try.'

We crossed the stateline into Nevada south of Gardnerville and swept north to Carson City. Just before the link route to Tahoe a Highway Patrol car overtook us. A burly man with a snapbrim hat was driving it. He didn't even look at us. After a few minutes a vintage Packard came the other way, its motor noisy with valve clatter and piston-slap. An old party with a goatee beard leaned out and yelled: 'They got a road block a couple miles ahead. If you folks don't want to be held up you'd better . . . '

He stopped simultaneously with his

242

motor and hopped out like a sprightly sparrow. I stopped, too. He had the bonnet of his old heap up and was poking around underneath it. Then he banged the lid down and wheezed: 'Plug lead come adrift. I fixed it.'

'What's the road block for?' I asked him.

He tugged at his wispy grey beard. 'Darned if I knows, young feller. They didn't say. Just looked at my licence and what-all. Looking for some murderer or bank robber, I shouldn't wonder.' His rheumy eyes surveyed us thoughtfully. 'I guess you ain't robbed a bank, eh?'

'Not lately,' I grinned.

He cackled wheezily. 'I can see you're a nice young feller,' he said. 'You don't want to be messed around by them cops.'

'Not really — we're anxious to get home.'

'And quite right, too. The way them police stop innocent citizens going about their lawful occasions is a public outrage, that's what.' He climbed back into the driving seat, yanked at the starter and the ancient motor clattered into life again.

'There's a lane on your left 'bout a quarter mile down the road. You take that is my advice, folks.'

'Thanks, dad.'

'Only too happy to oblige, son. Highway Patrol — bah!' He spat into the dust, let his clutch in with a bang and shot forward leaving a billow of exhaust fumes. They tasted fine.

A minute or so later I had found the lane and turned into it. 'If I knew his name and address I'd buy him a new car,' I said. 'I don't know if the Highway Patrol are looking for us, but running into that road block could have been awkward.'

'We crossed the stateline without anything happening . . . '

'Yeah, but that could have been luck. Anyway, we've dodged that block.'

The lane was narrow and tortuous, little more than a mule track — but it finally brought us back on the road well beyond the block point. I drove for several more miles, then left it. Time passed. The last rays of the dying sun tipped the distant peaks of the purple mountains, tinting them with sudden flecks of amber and glowing gold. A wind blew down through the tall timber and sagebrush, touching everything with the breath of the remote icy pools up in the High Sierras, slapping gently against the driving window.

Then we were in Virginia City, the old home town of the Comstock Lode, the town that yielded more than five hundred million dollars in gold and the same in silver up to the year World War II got under way, though the rip-roaring frontier days had ended long ago. Before the turn of the century forty thousand hard-bitten citizens with silver in their pants pockets and fire in their bellies went on a rampage that lasted all of four decades. Now something like a couple of thousand people live there, and the hell-to-breakfast shindig is a long-gone memory. For this is the ghost town of the West.

I had been there once before, searching for a tall blonde with twenty-five thousand dollars in a brown calfskin handbag. I found her in the end, but I never recovered the twenty-five thousand because the case wasn't anything it had seemed to be at the start. Still, I found her. I hoped to God I was going to find Julie . . . in time.

We drove down on to C Street past the boarded sidewalks fronting sagging frame buildings, breathing the dead air of disintegration and decay. Even the fantastic mansion which once had its door handles made of solid silver was crouched shabbily like an old, old man in a corner, no longer wanting to be reminded that he was once young and virile. As Comstock himself had been when he bought a wife from a Mormon for a horse, a gun and sixty dollars — only to lose her to a miner with a roving eye.

It was dark now, the heavy purple dark they have in these parts. The few people who were about moved softly and swiftly, like silent memories flitting through a lost world. Or is your imagination playing you tricks tonight, Shand?

Perhaps. After all, Virginia City was not totally devoid of contemporary amenities. They still had the Crystal Bar and it was open. There was a smaller one even closer and we went there first.

The bartender was a small man with a domed head on which no hair grew. He was wearing a shiny black suit with a shiny black cravat folded under a frayed cutaway collar and a watchchain big enough to tow the Queen Elizabeth into dock.

I was ordering the Bonanza Fizz which is still the local specialty when Annette shook her head. 'Orange juice,' she said.

'Sorry, I forgot. One Fizz, one orange juice.'

The bartender smiled against a mouthful of store teeth white as china dogs and set the drinks up. 'Don't get many strangers in town these days,' he offered conversationally.

I looked round. We were the only customers. He noticed and added: 'There'll be folks in later. It's kind of early.'

'There's still a silver pressure group here, isn't there?' I said.

'That's so. But there ain't so much silver to pressurize about.' He grinned.

I remembered that the group was run by a caucus of fourteen senators — but we weren't in this town of ghosts to talk about the Comstock Lode and the fortunes in silver that were now little more than a faded memory.

I bought him a drink and said: 'We're here on a brief visit, looking somebody up.'

'So?'

'The trouble is we've mislaid the address. Perhaps you can help us out?'

'I might, at that. I know 'most everybody round these parts. What name would it be?'

'O'Hara.'

He stared hard at me. 'Laird O'Hara, I guess you mean. Now that's funny.'

I gave him back his stare. 'What's funny about it?' I asked.

He fingered the ends of his cravat. 'Nobody ever asks about Laird O'Hara in a long whiles . . . but you're the second tonight.'

'Oh?'

'Yeah, a guy came in here earlier asking for him.' He took his hand away from his cravat and picked up his drink. He seemed to be thinking.

'Would you care for another drink?' I said.

'Why, that's real nice of you,' he replied. 'I believe I will.' He reached for the bottle and poured himself about three fingers.

I waited for him to go on. I had an odd feeling that he was trying to decide something in his mind. Finally, he looked hard at me again and said: 'You wouldn't be friends of his?'

'The man who came in here?'

He nodded. I said: 'So far as I know, we have no friends visiting here. What sort of man was he?'

The bartender leaned forward slightly. 'Well-dressed, white face, hard eyes. I didn't like his manner. More than that, I didn't like anything about him.' His voice was bitter.

'He's no friend of ours,' I said. 'What was wrong with his manner?'

'It was the way he spoke.'

'Arrogant?'

'Yeah, that's the word. I don't go for guys who come in my bar and treat me like I was the hired help.'

'He was alone then?'

'I didn't see anybody with him,' the bartender answered. 'But he had a car and could be there was someone in it. I didn't look.'

'And he wanted to find O'Hara, you say?'

The bartender grinned. 'Yeah, so I told him.'

'That was generous of you, wasn't it, after taking a dislike to him?'

'I told him the wrong address,' the bartender said. 'A disused log cabin five miles out of town, going south.'

I finished my drink and said: 'If he's mean he might come back to settle accounts with you.'

The bartender stooped a little, reaching below the counter. I watched him silently, then said: 'You've a gun down there, haven't you?'

'Yeah. Got me a sawed-off, and I knows how to use it. He better not come looking for trouble in here, mister.'

'Where does O'Hara live, or don't you want to tell us, either?'

He straightened-up, smiling. 'I'll tell

you, friend. He has a ramshackle old place just off this street. Turn right at the next intersection. It's about three minutes in your car. You can't miss it. A queer sort of place. Folks round here call it Bootleg Manor.'

I stared and he went on: 'Laird O'Hara is a character. You must know that.'

'I haven't seen him in a long time,' I said. 'I just thought of looking him up while we were here.'

'You're a friend from way back?'

'You could say that.'

He eyed me intently and said: 'You don't look old enough to remember him when . . . ' He hesitated and then added abruptly: 'Laird O'Hara used to be a big shot, if you know what I mean, but I guess that was long ago. Give him my regards when you see him.'

'I'll do that.'

'He don't come in here much these days,' the bartender said musingly. 'In fact, he don't leave that place of his hardly at all.'

'It sounds as if he's become a recluse.'

'He has his groceries and stuff

delivered and pays on the doorstep in cash . . . old dollar notes, very old notes. I never heard of him going to the bank.'

'Well, thanks,' I said.

We went out of the bar and got back in the car. I drove down the street and turned and found the place. It was a rambling old three-storey frame house with a rotting veranda set back from the sidewalk behind a garden in which a jungle of tousled grass grew two feet high except where it had been crudely scythed down over a weed-strewn path. There were lights in the house, all over the house, as if a big party was swinging, though I didn't think it was. Despite the lights, the whole place had the faded look of desolation.

I navigated my way up the path and climbed the four steps on to the veranda. A plank squeaked under my feet. The front door had a stained-glass panel of regrettable design let into it, and to the right of the door there was a tattered bell-rope. I pulled on it and cracked chimes whirred madly somewhere inside.

For a moment nothing happened. Then footsteps came down the hallway and the door opened and Laird O'Hara slammed a .45 Colt revolver in my chest.

22

He was a small man so far as height went, but what he lacked vertically he made up horizontally, nearly a Mr. Five-by-Five. His face was a collapsed ruin of sagging flesh and the hand which held the big gun was a fat ball, shining and veined like the hand of an old man — but it was rock-steady. The eyes were a hard unwinking blue under the puffed lids, yet in some paradoxical way were tinged with vagueness. He was wearing a crumpled double-breasted navy suit with a nipped-in waist and wide lapels and cuffed trouser bottoms. It must have been a fashionably sharp number in the Fall of 1932.

'Freeze the mitts, punk,' he said. His voice was high and thin like a twanged piano wire.

'What's the gun for, Mr. O'Hara?' I asked.

'One move is all you got to make,' he

answered. 'And that goes for the moll, too.'

'We're here as friends,' I said.

'Yeah?' He laughed. It sounded like a rough file rasping on tin. 'Friends is something I ran out of a long whiles back.'

I said patiently: 'Do we look like enemies, Mr. O'Hara?'

He peered at me, considering the point. 'Don't remember you,' he said uneasily.

'You never saw me before, that's why.' I told him who I was.

'That don't mean anything,' he said. 'You know who I am . . . I guess Al sent you, huh?'

'We're no friends of his,' I said.

'So you do know him?' His eyes, which had gone vague again, suddenly darted.

'We've seen him. A thin, white-faced fellow. He was with another fellow who got dead, a man called Ugo.'

O'Hara stared at us as if what I had said made no sense to him. 'Al's white-faced, but he ain't no skinny number . . .'

'He was when we saw him.'

'Don't play games with me,' he screeched. 'Capone's a fat guy, not so fat as me but fat.'

I gaped. 'Capone?'

'Yeah, the Big Shot.' He blinked rapidly. I wondered whether to make a grab for his gun, but thought better of it.

Instead, I said wonderingly: 'You're talking about Al Capone?'

'Who else?'

'Capone's dead,' I said.

That rocked him. He teetered back, passing his free hand over his face. But the other still held the gun.

'Dead . . . ' He mumbled the word stupidly. Then his eyes hardened again. 'Who give it to him? Machine Gun Jack McGurn . . . one of the O'Banions?'

'Capone got put away for tax evasion and died twenty years ago,' I said.

'Dead,' he said again. 'Nobody told me Al was dead.'

'I'm telling you, Mr. O'Hara.'

'How do I know he didn't send you here with this story just to fool me?' His eyes became suddenly cunning. 'It's a trick to throw me off my guard.'

'For God's sake, this is 1967,' I said. 'The Capone empire is nothing but a memory.'

'Says you.' He wagged the Colt at me. 'If Al's dead who's running the bootleg liquor business — tell me that!'

'Prohibition is dead, too, Mr. O'Hara. They repealed the Eighteenth Amendment a long, long time ago.'

'Repeal? You're crazy, they'd never do that!'

I thought Laird O'Hara was crazy, but I decided not to tell him. Perhaps he was only partially crazy. Perhaps there was another way of getting through to him. 'After Capone died The Syndicate took over, Mr. O'Hara. Right now there's a new outfit working for control. They call themselves The Organization ... ' I stopped because his strange eyes had become knowingly sane.

'The Organization ... that's right, a new mob. They ousted Dino and he aims to get even and take over himself.'

'Dino Carelli,' I said. 'This lady is his wife.'

He peered at her, his face a welter of thought.

'This is Annette Falaise, the singer who married Dino in Vegas,' I said.

He went on standing there, his eyes boring into her. Then, abruptly, he lowered the gun and said: 'You could of told me that first off . . . let's go inside and gargle.'

I started to say something, but he didn't wait. He turned and marched down a huge musty hallway and through an open door into a lounge cluttered with overstuffed furniture on a ripped and threadbare carpet which looked as if it could have been something special around the time when Daddy Browning and Peaches were making the headlines. There were vast armchairs and gaunt black settees with the horsehair seeping through jagged bursts in the cracked leather, spindle-legged chairs with the gilt flaking off them, upturned crates piled with forgotten debris, heavy blood-red velvet window drapes in the penultimate stages of dissolution, and angled across a corner of the room a massive curved bar stacked with liquor bottles.

'What'll it be, friends?' O'Hara intoned the words with a sort of mad jubilation. 'This calls for a celebration.'

'Scotch,' I said.

'The real stuff I got, not that bootleg rotgut for the suckers,' he cackled. 'No bathtub gin made by a mess of Sicilian alky-cookers — haw, haw!'

'I don't drink, Mr. O'Hara,' said Annette.

He spun round. 'You got to have one to celebrate your return, baby. Dino will be real pleased to see you.'

'She'll have one,' I said.

He went behind the bar and I whispered: 'You don't need to drink it. Just pretend. He'll never notice. You can pour it away when he isn't looking.'

'Dale,' she whispered, 'everything's gone mad.'

'Yeah, he's mixed-up in his mind, living in the past . . . but not all the time.'

There was a sudden dull plopping sound. I turned. Laird O'Hara had slammed a huge bowie-knife into the pitted top of the bar and was leaning on the handle. Another cackle came from him. 'I can use one of these faster'n you can shoot a gun,' he said. 'Dino, too.' A frown corrugated his lined forehead. 'Capone had better remember that,' he muttered.

'Tell us about Dino,' I said.

'Dino?' He repeated the name absently. Then his face cleared. He was back in the present. He was a well man again, or as well as he was ever going to be. 'Sure — Dino called me on the phone from some place down in Mexico. He's joining me here tonight.'

I felt Annette's hand close on mine. I wrapped fingers round it with my other hand, pressing hard. She stayed silent.

'The Organization are after him,' I said.

'They are?' He wound both his hands round the handle of the big knife. 'They better not come here.'

'A man named Al — another Al, nothing to do with Capone — is on his way here, Mr. O'Hara. He's been trying to locate you.'

There was no longer any vagueness in his manner now. The eyes which looked down at us from behind the bar were cold and glittering. 'Dino warned me somebody might try to bump me off,' he said. 'I thought at first you was them.'

'We're not, Mr. O'Hara. These men are after us as well.'

He nodded, reached down and came up with a Thompson sub-machine gun, *circa* 1928. 'Then we'll kind of get set for a cosy party,' he said.

I went across to the tall window and looked out through a wide slit in the velvet drapes. The street was empty.

O'Hara roared: 'Let 'em come . . . I'll blast 'em the second they come through the door.' His shaggy eyebrows drew together. 'You ain't said who you are,' he accused.

'The name is Shand — Dale Shand.'

'Yeah? What're you doing going around with Dino's girl?'

'The Organization kidnapped her. I was able to get her away from them.'

'So? Dino will be pleased to know that. Yessir, Dino will be real pleased.' He laid the machine gun on the bar, but kept one hand close to it. He had forgotten about the drinks. His eyes were clouding again.

I said sharply: 'You say Dino will be here tonight?'

That jerked him back. 'Sometime tonight. Or maybe early tomorrow. I'm not sure. But he's coming. He has to see me. He needs me.'

I wrestled with thoughts. Finally, I said: 'Why does he need you?'

'I got some information for him, Shand.'

'Information about what?'

'You'd like to know, wouldn't you?' he said craftily.

'We're friends, Mr. O'Hara. I saved his wife.'

'That's so, but . . . ' He seemed to hesitate, then went on: 'It's about the big fellow Dino's after, the guy who's set up The Organization.'

I lit a cigarette and dragged on it. The smoke felt raw against my palate. 'How do you know about The Organization?' I said.

'I was in Chicago two-three weeks ago. I found something out. Something about him.'

'The man who calls everybody *amico*?'

His strange eyes flickered again. 'That's him, Shand.'

'You know him?'

'I never met him, no. But I heard something about him. I was in a place, a little place down on State Street, one of them places where you could have a room and a girl.' He grinned. 'I'm getting too old for that, and besides the place ain't like that now. But I knew it from way back, so I went in for a drink and . . . ' He paused, as if the effort of concentration was too much.

'You went to this place for a drink and what happened?' I prompted.

Laird O'Hara shook himself. 'What place was that?'

'A place on State Street in Chicago.'

'Yeah, that's right, it was. I almost forgot. A place on State Street . . . Larry's Bar they call it now. I found out something . . . '

'Something about Johnny Cassatta?'

Suddenly, he was more than wide awake, no longer even remotely muddled. 'That's a dangerous name, Shand,' he said. 'If you're in with Cassatta . . . ' His fingers twitched on the stock of the machine gun.

'I don't know him, Mr. O'Hara. I heard the name, just like you heard it.'

'Oh? Well, that's diff'rent.' His face smiled happily. 'And you're a friend of Dino's. Well, I found out something, something which will help Dino.'

'Why didn't you tell him when he called you from Mexico?'

'I forgot it. I forget things times. Besides, Dino thought it better not to say anything over the phone. He said he was coming here. Then I remembered what it was and I'm gonna tell him when . . . ' He broke off, his entire body stiffening. 'Somebody's coming up to the house,' he whispered.

I took my automatic out. O'Hara picked up the machine gun and aimed it at the doorway. There was a silence, a massive silence like something you could reach out and touch.

'Stay out of this, Annette,' I said. 'You'd better . . . '

O'Hara interrupted. 'She can duck

down behind the bar, she'll be safe there. I don't want nothing to happen to Dino's girl.'

She moved round the overstuffed furniture as the cracked chimes whirred. I looked questioningly at Laird O'Hara. He nodded. I went fast across the room and down the hallway and held the front door open and stood behind it. There was no sound, no movement.

'You can come in,' I said.

For a moment he still didn't move. Then he stepped carefully forward, enough for me to see him as he came — behind a long silenced gun.

I brought my automatic down with a hard chop on the base of his neck and he shot forward. The long gun jumped out of his hand. I kicked it across the hall and stood over him. He was Al.

'The girl,' I snarled. 'The girl you forced into your car at Crestview . . . where is she?'

He rolled over. I stood back while he crawled painfully on to his hands and knees. There was a thin trickle of blood on his collar and his neck was swelling, but he wasn't badly hurt. His face glared whitely under the lights.

'I'll ask one more time,' I said. 'After that you get it.'

His lips moved, framing croaked words. 'You're Dale Shand . . . '

I aimed the gun down at him. His mouth twisted. 'If you kill me you'll never know,' he said.

'You've got five seconds to talk.'

He looked at the gun, then up at me. 'She isn't here,' he said. 'You got to believe that. I handed her over. She's in Chicago. If you want to see her alive again you better go there with me.'

'You're looking at a gun,' I said harshly.

'It makes no difference, Shand. You want to see her again you come back with me . . . '

'Where is she in Chicago?'

'I don't know where they're holding her, but if you come back with me she'll be handed over. They are going to contact you . . . '

'How?'

'They got men looking out for you, Shand. There's a lot of ways and . . . '

I said: 'Get up!'

He came back on his feet. He put fingers up gingerly to touch the swollen tissue on his neck, pulled them away and looked at the blood. 'I didn't figure on you being here, Shand,' he said. 'I was looking for someone else . . . '

'Dino Carelli.'

'Yeah, we figure he's here, with O'Hara, they're friends.'

'He isn't here, not yet. What's your name?'

'Al Zurke.' He eyed me without expression. 'Ugo got killed on the Yosemite Falls on account of you warned Dino's wife.' He shrugged. 'So I made your girl come with me. Well, she's been driven to Chicago. You want to see her you come with me. That gun you're holding ain't going to help you. It's the perfect stand-off, gumshoe . . . '

He stopped, half-turning. Laird O'Hara had come through the lounge doorway. His eyes weren't clouded, but they were still half-crazed.

'Heard what you said, Zurke,' he whispered. 'You came for me and Dino . . . yeah, Dino said somebody'd come and told me to watch out . . . '

A laugh welled from him, like no laugh I had ever heard. He had the Thompson sub-machine gun in the crook of his arm, triggering it as the mad laugh faded.

A hail of bullets almost tore Al Zurke apart. He lurched, spun completely round and reeled down the enormous hallway. O'Hara was still raking him from head to foot. He crashed through the open door, jerking like a tormented puppet, went down on the tangled path, rolling over and over.

A car slewed to a stop and the driver leaped out with a gun pointing. I dived behind the door, yelling to O'Hara but he went on walking down the hallway. There was a hard, snapping blast.

Laird O'Hara dropped the machine gun. For a split second he stood still, a surprised look on his face. Then he went slowly down on his huge knees and put his gross face in the floor.

Dino Carelli came up the path.

I stepped out from the door.

'You've just killed the wrong man,' I said.

23

It stopped him in his tracks. The big shambling body was partly hunched forward. His gun was jutting out, but he didn't try to use it. He was looking at mine.

'You!' He glared at me. 'So you've been tailing me all the time, whoever you are.'

'No,' I said. 'I haven't been looking for you, Carelli. I came here for something else. You could describe it as rather a long story.'

'I ought to kill you, fellow.'

'The way things look just at this moment, we might easily kill each other,' I said. 'Suppose we don't even try?'

He went on glaring at me. Then, suddenly, he shrugged. 'Okay, so it's checkmate.' He thrust his gun back in its shoulder-clip, watched me put mine up and said: 'What did you mean about I just killed the wrong man?'

'O'Hara,' I said. 'He was coming down

the hallway and you shot him.'

He staggered back as if a door had been slammed in his face. When he spoke again his voice was a croak. 'Jesus . . . I didn't know . . . I saw this fellow come through the door and I'd heard the shooting and I just fired . . . '

'You're too trigger-happy, Carelli.' I stood aside and he came into the hallway and stared down at Laird O'Hara. Then a surprising thing happened. He went down on one knee, cradled O'Hara in his arms and shook with sobs.

'I killed him . . . Christ, I killed him . . . '

The bullet had gone into O'Hara's chest at heart level. A shot fired almost blindly by a man too quick with a gun. Almost an accidental shot. He hadn't wanted to kill O'Hara. They were friends. But it made no difference. Laird O'Hara was dead and whatever he had been going to tell Dino Carelli had died with him.

Carelli let the lifeless body slip gently to the floor. He stood up, blinking and passed a hand across his eyes.

I said: 'O'Hara told me he had some

information for you, something important. No, he didn't say what it was, except that it had to do with a man who used to be known as Johnny Cassatta.'

'You know too much, fellow.'

'All I know is that a syndicate calling itself The Organization kidnapped me because I saw you kill that guy in L.A.,' I said patiently.

He looked fixedly at me. Then he said: 'You levelling?'

'They thought I knew where to locate you,' I answered. 'When they found that I didn't and that I saw it merely by chance they were going to kill me. I made a getaway, but they're still after me . . . just as they're still looking for you, Carelli.'

'Yeah?' He grinned wolfishly. 'I'm looking for *them*.' His eyes flickered. 'How do you know my name?'

'They told me,' I said. It was both true and misleading, but I didn't want to tell him about Annette. I wondered what she was doing.

He took a cigarette from his shirt pocket and lit it, dragging deeply on the smoke. 'Who *are* you?' he asked.

I told him. I told him something of what had been happening. It sounded less than convincing because I had to leave Annette out of it.

'It doesn't figure,' he said harshly. 'Why should you chase around the country after this mob? You don't have a real reason. There has to be something else . . . ' A faint rustle sounded behind him and he spun round. 'Annette!'

She was standing in the doorway of the lounge. The trembling apprehension which had possessed her when she saw him in the bar had gone. She was white, but her voice was steady.

'Hello, Dino,' she said.

'Baby . . . I missed you so.'

'You never missed me, Dino. You were already through with me. You were cheating on me even before the police arrested you. You never missed anything except your liberty . . . and all the easy money.'

'We had something once,' he said. 'It could be like that again.'

'No,' she answered. 'No, this time *I'm* through.'

He turned slowly toward me and said: 'What's she doing with you, Shand?'

'He saved my life,' she said quietly.

'Yeah? He carefully didn't tell me you were here.'

She went on as if he hadn't spoken. 'I was in that bar when you came down. I knew you hadn't seen me and I didn't want you to. It's all over between us, long over. I was scared of meeting you, scared of reopening everything. So I ran out. Dale covered me.'

He looked at the cigarette burning low between his fingers and stubbed it out. 'I guess I mistreated you, baby,' he said.

'I didn't have a very nice life with you, Dino. I was frightened of it starting up again.'

Carelli looked at me and said: 'I thought there was a woman in that bar, it was just a fleeting impression I got. So you stood in the line of vision while she left?'

'That was how I got into it,' I said. 'But that was only the beginning. The Organization knew I was there. They were watching at the front. They saw Annette go in, but they didn't know she'd gone out the rear exit. They decided that she knew where you could be found.'

He blew air quickly through his lips and said: 'They'd torture her if they caught-up with her.'

'Yes.'

'What did you mean about Shand saving your life?' he asked her.

'After I left the bar I was still frightened that you'd find me. Dale discovered where I'd gone and followed to warn me about The Organization.'

She paused and glanced at me. I told him the rest of it.

'And now they've got your girl,' he said. 'That's bad.'

'I'm going after her,' I said. 'If I can't do it any other way I'll have to give myself up to them. They won't do anything to her, not yet.'

'They'll kill you, Shand.'

'I said if there's no other way.'

He stood there, a big shambling man with his long arms hanging down at his sides. His craggy face, no longer carrying a jail pallor, looked almost friendly.

'I wish you luck,' he said. 'Where are you going to start looking?'

'Chicago. She'll be there. O'Hara told me The Organization are there, or some of them. I'll try to find where they are — unless they find me first.'

'It's not much to go on, Shand.'

'It'll have to do.' I hadn't told him about Larry's Bar — the one thing I had to go on. Instead, I said: 'Johnny Cassatta is the head man — but the name is a front, isn't it?'

'Yeah.'

'O'Hara hinted that he knew who Cassatta really is, or has become.'

'He was going to tell me,' Carelli said. 'For God's sake, why did I have to shoot him?'

'It was an accident.'

He made a brittle laugh. 'The cops won't believe that . . . ' He stopped as if an uneasy thought had come to him. 'It's funny they ain't shown. The gunfire . . . somebody must've heard it.'

'This house stands on its own, the rest of the street is just old warehouses,' I said. 'If anybody heard it would be distantly.

Just the same, somebody's bound to come along, and soon.'

He nodded. 'I'm blowing, Shand. I don't like leaving the Laird here, but I guess they'll give him a decent burial and . . . '

Carelli stopped again. A siren was wailing, some way off, but it was coming nearer. 'Someone heard the shots all right and the cops is looking,' he said. 'So long, Shand . . . and good-bye, baby.'

He ran down the path and got in his car and started driving. Less than a minute later we were in ours. The siren was still wailing, but the prowl car wasn't in sight — yet. I drove down small dark streets on sidelights, finally drifted out on to the glossy highway which spans, in a series of curves, the twenty-three miles of sagebrush between Virginia City and Reno. Nobody came after us. The road was almost deserted.

Annette was strangely silent. We were more than halfway there before she spoke. 'What are you going to do, Dale?'

'I've already said — I'll find Julie or take my chance with the mob.'

'You're a very brave man,' she said.

'I'm frightened, Annette, the way any man can be frightened, no matter how he pretends. But I can't leave her to them, I *can't*.'

'And me?'

'I'm putting you on a flight back to Los Angeles. I'll call Captain Logan and explain.'

'No,' she said militantly. 'I'm coming with you.'

'I can't let you do it, Annette. Another thing — I'll have a better chance trying to work this out alone. A man and a woman going around together are more conspicuous.'

'I . . . suppose so.'

'It's not supposition. Don't make it tougher for me than it already is.'

'But . . . '

'No, don't argue, for God's sake. Do what I tell you.'

'All right,' she said.

I ran the car on to the airport parking lot and walked with her into the main building. A television monitor screen showed a flight to Los Angeles at 19.00

hours. Exactly fifty minutes from now. There were vacant seats and I bought her a ticket and she checked-in. The flight was called and I walked with her through the departure lounge and up to the flight gate.

Suddenly, with tears streaming down her face, she flung herself into my arms. Then she stood back, both hands still holding me.

'Bless you, Dale,' she whispered. She lifted her hands to my face, pulled me towards her and kissed me. Then she turned and was gone.

I went back to the booking counter and bought a single ticket to Chicago. The plane was scheduled to take-off in thirty minutes. I had time to call Logan. I hoped he was in.

24

He was. A routine voice on the switchboard said: 'What name, please?'

'I'll tell him myself. Just say it's important.'

'Hold on and I'll see if the captain will take the call.' There was a small interval, then I was through.

'Logan, captain of detectives, Central Homicide,' he said. 'Who's calling?'

'Shand.'

'Good evening, Mr. Shand. So you're back?'

'No, I'm in Reno.'

He didn't yell down the line like Hammer. He chuckled. 'Reno, eh? You getting a divorce?'

'I'm not married, captain, though I'm with a lady — or was. Annette Falaise.'

'So you finally found her?'

'Yes. I'd better explain.'

'It's an idea,' he said dryly.

'First, I'm at the airport here. She's just

left on the 19.00 hours flight to Los Angeles. Will you meet the plane?'

'We'll do that.' He paused and went on: 'As I recall it, your undertaking to Lieutenant Hammer was that if you found her you would bring her back yourself.'

'Yes, but something else has happened.'

'Tell it,' he said tersely. He listened without interruption. Then he said: 'You can't handle a thing like this alone, Shand.'

'I have to, captain. Show me any other way.'

'The police in Chicago ought to be told.'

'That could be signing her death warrant.'

Logan said quietly: 'As a police officer I don't like it that a private investigator is trying to do police work.'

'I'm not asking you to like it, captain. I don't like it myself. But I have to do it.'

'You've no guarantee that I won't contact the Chicago police the moment you get off the line,' he said.

'No, but it won't help them if they

don't know where to look.'

'I imagine they're not without resources,' he said soberly.

'They still need to know where to start looking, and they don't.'

'Meaning that you do?'

'Yes. It's the one thing I'm holding back — nothing else.'

'I'm going to have to tell them, just the same.'

'I can't stop you. I had to make this call, though. But for the need to protect Miss Falaise I probably wouldn't have done.'

'You gave us an undertaking. Remember?'

'And I'd have kept it but for what's arisen. Are you going to slap a charge on me?'

'No.' he answered coolly. 'I guess we could, but I'm not doing it. I've had a conference with the D.A. about you. We don't think you killed the man in the hotel. We're quite sure you have no part in The Organization. In fact, we're willing to give you a clean bill of health — apart from the trouble you've caused us by failing to show for the coroner's inquiry.' He made another chuckle. 'Lieutenant Hammer doesn't quite agree with us. In fact, he'd like to throw the book at you. By the way, we found that rented house in Beverly Hills. The occupants had blown all right.'

'Leaving no clues, I imagine.'

'Nothing — but we found that the house was rented through an agency in New York.'

'Everything seems to point back to New York,' I said. 'What agency?'

'West Coast Buildings and Leases, with an address on Fourteenth Street.,'

'I'll bet they're no longer in business there.'

'It was just an accommodation address. We checked it out. No such company registered. I'd say the place only existed to negotiate the tenancy of the house — and that it was a front for the man or men who took over the house. When you escaped they closed down the accommodation address, if they hadn't already done it.'

'I know Captain Magulies of the New

York Police Department,' I said slowly. 'He might be able to help you.'

'I've been through to him. That's how we got this information. He's still making inquiries. Incidentally, I told him about you.'

'I hope he gave me a clean bill of health, too.'

'He said you were inclined to be both obstinate and difficult, have been known to hold out on the police to protect a client, but that you were an honest man and that he usually let you have a little rope. I'm doing the same — except for one modification. I'm going to call Chicago. Maybe the law there can help more than you think.'

'I can't prevent you, captain. But, equally, I can't see my way to telling you where I'm going when I get there.'

'It might be better, Shand.'

'I can't take the risk.'

'All right, if that's the way it has to be. I'll ask them to check on any known or suspected members of The Organization in Chicago, proceeding with caution, as we say. One thing I'll do for you — I won't have them meet your plane when it lands.'

'Thanks.'

'That's all right. Oh — and we still want you back in L.A.'

'I'll come — if I'm still alive,' I said.

I put the phone down, picked up my case and walked through the barrier and down a white-walled corridor and out to the waiting plane. The night was heavy with warmth, but suddenly I felt cold and tired and more than half-way to being ill. I slung my case in the baggage rack and bought a drink. It didn't help. A stewardess asked if I wanted dinner. I shook my head. It seemed to be full of cottonwool. Thoughts flitted uneasily through it, but they made no pattern, offered no pointer to action. I was going to Chicago to find men I had never seen, unknown men holding a girl prisoner in a house, a hotel room, a cellar . . . anywhere in a great sprawling city of millions. I could see her face, could almost feel the warmth of her body against mine. I was going to Chicago to find her and all I had to go on was the name of a bar on State Street. I was going to Chicago with a hope so tenuous that it only just existed.

But it was a hope and it was all I had.

25

I walked off the plane. I was still cold, but now the waiting was over and I had something to do. I was in Chicago and Julie was there, somewhere. I was going to find her. I *had* to find her.

A taxi took me fast down the freeway. I had been here before, a long time ago. A great city to be in, if you weren't tortured by thoughts and fears and hopes. New Michigan Avenue and the Union Stockyards, the Edgewater Beach Hotel and the dark slum sprawl of the South Side. The Loop and the plaza at Grant Park, the sixty-eight windows of the Marshall Field store — perhaps they have more now, but the girl clerks would still look like reigning beauty queens. Lakeshore winds blowing down the boulevards, pleasure boats far out on the vast deeps of Lake Michigan, the interurban trains honking their horns on the Illinois Central . . . and the latter-day disciples of

Bugs Moran and Schemer Drucci and Machine-Gun Jack McGurn adding their unhumble quota to the city's five million dollar crime bill — maybe it was up to ten million now? Among the disciples would be the men who held Julie Arden. I was on my way to meet them.

We went south on Wabash Avenue past the spot where, long ago, Big Jim Colosimo had a restaurant from which he controlled a chain of joy houses yielding a gross revenue of more than three hundred thousand dollars a year. On past Twenty-ninth and Dearborn, finally to the intersection of State and Twenty-second where Al Capone, lording it in the Lexington Hotel, grossed eighteen million dollars annually from bootleg liquor. But that was long ago, too, except in the half-crazed mind of Laird O'Hara, and now he was gone.

I found Larry's Bar. A neon sign spelled its name in emerald green letters on a crescent over the entrance. No steps. You walked straight in off the street. It wasn't large and the lighting was dim. Quiet booths were ranged against one wall. The bar counter faced the booths and a slim boy in a white mess jacket stood behind it. The place was more than half-empty. I looked round, trying to make the look casual. There were several couples in the booths. None of them looked dangerous. I sat on a high stool against the bar and ordered Scotch.

'On the rocks, sir?'

'No, thanks, just water.'

A man sat next to me, a man with a sad face and a long white nose. He had a pile of small change on the bar and looked as if he was drinking his way through it until it was time to go home for the showdown. He didn't look dangerous, either.

The bartender slid my drink across. He was about twenty-five, with a smooth face and pale blue eyes starting to look tired, as though he had been there too long.

'Nice place you have here,' I said.

'Thanks. I haven't seen you in here before, have I, sir?'

'No, I didn't know about it. A friend told me.'

He smiled, a polite professional smile as tired as his eyes.

'That's right, he told me to be sure to stop by for a drink.'

'Well, the liquor here is good, better than some places.' He picked up a soft damp cloth and began polishing the spotless counter.

'So I heard, that's why I came in — that and to meet a friend.' I nursed my drink and said: 'It looks like he's late . . . '

'Too bad, sir.'

I glanced ostentatiously at my watch. 'I was a trifle late getting here myself. Maybe he's been and gone.'

'One or two customers left recently,' the boy said. 'Maybe I'd know your friend if you told me his name. Some of them I know by name.'

'Johnny Cassatta,' I said.

He didn't react. If the name meant anything to him he was masking it with an actor's ease. 'Don't know that name, sir,' he said. 'I'm sorry.'

'Well, it was just a chance,' I replied.

Two men came in and called noisily for service. The man with the sad face suddenly quit drinking. He picked up his pile of dimes, slid quietly off his stool and went quietly across the floor. He didn't speak, didn't turn. He just went across the dim bar and out on to the street and there was nothing odd about it . . . except that he had left his last drink untasted.

I was out on the sidewalk in time to see him moving fast down the street. It was crowded and I could follow him without much risk of being seen. He didn't go far, not more than fifty yards to a pay telephone booth. He had got the door open and had wedged himself inside as I came near. I had a sudden premonition that he was going to turn. I ducked low and went round the other side of the booth. He had made the turn and was looking back along the sidewalk so that he could see the entrance to the bar.

He had the receiver off its rest and began dialling. I read the number as he spun the digits. He got his connection and began speaking. I couldn't hear anything he said, but it didn't matter. I backed away from the booth, watching him all the time. But he was still looking carefully the other way, making sure he didn't miss anyone coming out of the bar.

I grinned, turned and vanished in the crowd. I walked on to the next intersection, went down it and found another telephone booth. It took me at least five minutes to check through the numbers until I found the one he had dialled — and the address that went with it. It was 2878a North Clark Street, the street where the Prohibition barons had their big kill on St. Valentine's Day back in 1929. It seemed an appropriate setting.

I went there in a taxi — but not quite all the way. I stopped it short and walked the rest. It was a faded office front aching for paint. The windows were heavy with the dust of years and one was partly boarded-up. A sign above the windows announced; *Chicago Trucking Co., Inc.* It looked as if it had been there since 1929. I walked straight past it without slackening my stride. There was a narrow alley between the building and the next one. I went down it, very slowly so that my eyes had time to adjust to the nearly opaque darkness, enough to see. The alley merged with another which spanned the rear of the block. I turned right and found a crumbling wall with a door let in it. The door was bolted. I jumped, clawing at the top of the wall, and hauled myself up. Below me on the other side was a square paved yard strewn with garbage bins and old packing crates. I lowered myself carefully down the other side of the wall until I judged that my feet were no more than inches from the ground. Then I let go. If I dropped on anything metallic they would almost certainly hear it.

Instead, I dropped squashingly on a pile of old rags. I moved off them with both hands extended, probing for the wall door. I found it and slid the bolt back and eased the door open wide enough to get through in a hurry if I had to. Then I turned back and started down the paved yard.

The rear door was locked. To the right of it was an undraped window. No light showed inside. Maybe there was nobody around? But Sad Face had called a number and this was the place he had called. I went back to the door, took out a small section of celluloid and inserted it in the lock, using gentle pressure. The wards turned with no more than a faint click. I put my shoulder to the panelling. The door hadn't been bolted — it opened inwards virtually without sound.

My heartbeats felt like sledgehammer blows and the back of my neck was as wet as a dog's nose, but I went in. Nobody sapped me down. I found a slim corridor with a door at the other end and finger-tipped it open, enough to slide round it. I was in the front office. Street lamps shone through the dusty windows. The lights showed me a room with some cheap basic furniture which looked as if it had been bought as a job lot in a junk store. Nothing else. No ring of hard-faced men glaring at me over their tommy guns. A bare desk, a faded grey steel filing cabinet and a square of indeterminate carpet. On the desk a telephone.

I stood in the middle of the silent room listening to my thoughts. They didn't amount to anything. This was the address Sad Face had called, it had to be — yet there was no one here, unless they were hiding. I opened a closet door, went out into the corridor and found some stairs and climbed them. The room above was as barren as a cut-rate insurance salesman's promises. I went back into the office. Nothing was making any sense. This was the place and somebody must have been here to take the call. They couldn't know I was coming, so maybe they had gone. But I still didn't like it, I didn't like anything about it. There was something wrong about the whole set-up. I put a cigarette in my mouth and scraped a match for it, staring at the telephone.

Then I saw it — the small thing I ought to have seen before. It was set in the desk at the base of the telephone and switched it through to another place when the office wasn't in use. I let the dying match flame drop to the floor and lifted the receiver.

A voice said yes with a question-mark.

'Hello, Malone,' I said softly.

A pause. Then, carefully, he said: 'Who's speaking?'

'Shand.'

Another pause.

His schooled voice came back. 'You are

clever, my friend. You have found out about our office — or one of them. A call to any one of the numbers comes through here when the offices are not in occupation.'

'I'm *in* one of the offices, Malone.'

'So? Ve-ry clever, Shand. But we knew you were in Chicago.'

'That was easy,' I sneered. 'The man who was in Larry's Bar told you. I watched the number he dialled.'

'And he didn't observe you? That was remiss of him.'

'He was looking the wrong way, in case I came out of the bar while he was making the call. He didn't know I'd already followed him.'

'But he should have known. We shall have to speak to him about it. Alberto is only a minor cog in The Organization, but even minor cogs must function smoothly. He was not in that bar by accident, Mr. Shand.'

'Don't tell me he was expecting me to show.'

'No, not you. Somebody else.'

'Somebody like Laird O'Hara?'

The bantering tone left his voice. 'We know he was there recently. He might come back, so we had the place staked out.'

'O'Hara found something out when he was there before,' I said.

'So you have seen O'Hara, Mr. Shand. I hope for your sake that he was not communicative.' There was a sudden sharp edge to Malone's speech.

'You sent one of your trouble boys to see if he was still in Virginia City,' I said. 'A man called Al. He's dead. O'Hara filled him full of machine-gun bullets.'

The line seemed to go dead. Then his voice was back, tight but under control. 'I see. And you were there.'

'I was there, Malone.'

'Interesting.'

'Dangerous, too?'

'Possibly. That will depend on how much or how little O'Hara told you.'

'You sent Al there to silence him when you realized he had found something . . . something about who Johnny Cassatta is.'

Malone made a small sound, a small

sound like expelled air. Then he said: 'What do you want, Mr. Shand?'

'The girl your hired mugs forced into a car at Crestview.'

'Ah, the charming Miss Arden. She is in safe keeping.'

'She knows nothing about Dino Carelli,' I snarled.

'We are aware of that, Mr. Shand. But she has another value.'

'If anything is done to her, Malone, I'll kill you — and the man behind your syndicate.'

'She will be freed — unharmed — when you deliver yourself to us, Mr. Shand. We could, to be sure, hunt you down. We have the means.'

'You haven't been too successful so far.'

'Nevertheless, we could do it — do not harbour any illusions on that score, my friend. But why should we go to all the trouble? We have the trump card . . . and you know it. Miss Arden will be released the moment you surrender yourself to us. I promise it. By the way, Miss Falaisc — where is she?'

'I lost her.'

'That is unfortunate, Mr. Shand. But the offer stands. You have twelve hours in which to decide.'

'Why the time lag?'

'We are generous men, Mr. Shand. Also' — he chuckled amusedly — 'we are attracted by the notion of your having ample time to ponder the high cost of refusal.'

'Where do you want me to be?'

'Where you are right now, my friend. You will return there in twelve hours from now and Miss Arden will be released in your presence.'

I put the phone down and stood there thinking. They were thoughts stripped of every last vestige of hope. The Organization would kill me, perhaps not quickly. All I had in return was a promise that was worth . . . how much?

A car came down the street and it suddenly occurred to me that they might not even wait for me to decide. I looked down through the window, but the car didn't stop. Just the same, it would be better not to stay here. I went out the way

I had come in, walked back along the alley and round into the street.

A girl was standing outside the dilapidated office. She was trying the door.

26

When she heard me she started violently and turned. She had a slightly flamboyant prettiness. The eyes that looked at me were wide and blue. They were also frightened.

'There isn't anyone in there,' I said.

'Who are you?' she whispered.

'Not one of them.'

'Oh!' The frightened look faded. She shrugged and said: 'I thought perhaps someone might be in. Well, good night . . . '

She turned to go. I said: 'Do you mind if I walk with you?'

Her face went tight. 'Don't get wrong ideas . . . ' she began.

'It's all right, I'm not trying to make you. I thought you might be able to tell me something about them.'

'I . . . I don't know what you're talking about,' she said uneasily.

'I'm trying to contact the men who

own this place. You may be able to help.'

'Look, I don't know you, I never saw you before. Why should I talk to you?'

'No reason, except that it's just possible we might have something in common.'

'I don't understand what that means.'

'We're both trying to contact them.'

'Who are you?' she said again.

'Just a man who wants some information. We might be able to help each other.'

She didn't answer immediately. Instead, she started walking. We went along the street and turned down another. 'I'd like a drink,' she said. 'There's a bar just ahead.'

We went in and sat facing each other in a booth. 'Gin,' she said.

I ordered a gin and a Scotch. The waiter brought them and drifted away.

'You still haven't said who you are . . . '

'The name is Shand.' I picked up my drink and added: 'You've heard it, haven't you?'

Her face had gone white. She nodded and started reaching for her handbag. It fell on the table between us. The clasp snapped open and I could see inside.

301

There was an automatic pistol in it, about .25 calibre, with an ivory grip. She stood up.

'Sit down!' I snarled.

She closed the bag, hugging it against her. But she sat down again.

'What's the gun for?'

'I . . . I just carry one. It's nothing to you.'

'Look,' I said, 'you were trying to get into that office and apparently thought you needed a weapon. It begins to seem that we might have something very much in common.'

'They'd kill me if they thought I was talking with you, Mr. Shand,' she said in a low voice.

'In that case, we won't tell them.'

She sat there looking at me as if she were trying to make up her mind. Then she said: 'I can't talk to you here, we might be seen.'

'We might be seen walking.'

'You look all right, Mr. Shand. Ask the bartender to call a taxi. We'll go to my apartment.'

He got one in minutes and we went

there. It was a private entrance apartment not more than a dozen blocks going south. She got lights on and walked through to the lounge, a wide room bright with colour and contemporary furniture.

She made two drinks in tall, misted glasses and said over her shoulder: 'Just what is it you want to know?'

'Your name, for a start.'

'Georgia Schutt.'

'How do you come to know these men, Miss Schutt?'

'I'm Frank Malone's girl.' Her long mouth closed in a bitter line. 'Or I was.'

I didn't say anything and she went on harshly: 'That's why I went to that office, to try to see him. I thought he might be there.'

'I had the same idea, but he wasn't.'

'How did you get in?'

'Burglarious entry is the legal definition.'

'And now you want me to tell you where he is?'

'If you went there looking for him I guess you don't know.'

'Oh, yes, I know, Mr. Shand. I mean I

know where he lives. I went to that office because they wouldn't let me see him at his apartment.' She drank some of her drink and went on: 'He said he was through with me. I kept trying to see him, but they threw me out. I thought he might go to that office, so I went there.'

'With an automatic pistol.'

'I was going to kill him,' she said calmly.

'He's not worth it, Georgia.'

'No? He had me thrown out — I mean literally thrown out.'

'It's still not worth a life sentence.'

'I know that, Mr. Shand. But knowing something doesn't necessarily help.'

'If he had been there he might have killed *you*.'

'I suppose so.' She smiled faintly. 'Anyway, I don't imagine I'll try to do it now.'

'Why did Malone throw you out?'

'The usual reason. He's got another girl. He denied it, but he's lying. She's been in his apartment. I caught a glimpse of her.'

I could feel the muscles of my face

tightening. 'Describe her,' I said.

'Why, what's it to you?'

'Please tell me what she looks like, Georgia.'

'Tall, a looker, coppery hair . . . ' She stared at me and added: 'What's the matter?'

'She's not his girl,' I said. 'She's being held against her will. That's why I was looking for him.'

I told her enough for her to understand. She said: 'So he just threw me out, anyway.'

'Yes, unless . . . ' But I couldn't face putting the thought into words.

Georgia Schutt did it for me. 'Unless he's forced himself on her . . . in which case you'll kill him.'

'Yes.' I could feel my fingernails grinding into my palms.

'But if they've kidnapped her as a kind of hostage he daren't do anything to her,' Georgia said. 'Frank's a big man in The Organization, but he isn't the biggest.'

'Who is?'

'I don't know. I've never seen him.'

'A man who used to be known as

Johnny Cassatta,' I said. 'But that was a long time ago and he has another name and probably doesn't even look quite the same.'

'What does it matter?' she asked. 'It's your girl you want, not him.'

'Yeah. Where does Frank Malone live?'

'He has an apartment on Lakeshore Drive. But it's too late . . . '

I stared.

'She isn't there, Mr. Shand.'

I gripped her arm savagely. 'What are you trying to say, Georgia?'

'You're hurting me,' she said.

'I'm sorry.' I let go.

'She's gone to New York. She went in a car with Haggart and Delmar, two of his boys. He's following — ' She stopped suddenly. 'Did Frank tell you she was still in Chicago?'

I nodded.

'That means they never had the smallest intention of letting her go,' Georgia said. 'And you were going to give yourself up to them . . . '

'That's what he hopes.'

'But you *were* going to, weren't you?'

'He gave me twelve hours. He liked the idea of my being stretched on a rack mentally. I was going to use the time — or try to.'

'Suppose you fail?'

'The rack won't be just a mental one. They have a score to settle with me and they won't hurry it.'

'But you haven't done anything.'

'I've done plenty they don't really know about. But, even apart from that, you're missing the point, Georgia. I'm the only outsider who has heard the voice of the man who controls The Organization. I would know it anywhere. That alone makes me too dangerous to go on living.'

'But they've given you twelve hours. You could talk to people, the police . . . '

'I can't tell them anything that would identify Johnny Cassatta. He's become another personality — a new name, a new life. It's much more than possible that he has a solid, respectable front. Also, he's operating from New York and that's where I live. The danger, from their point of view, is that I might meet him and recognize his voice.'

'Yes,' she said slowly. 'Yes, I can see it now.'

'O'Hara discovered something, by chance when he went into Larry's Bar. They were going to kill him. Only, by an ironic mischance, Dino Carelli unintentionally did it for them. That leaves only me to silence.'

'What are you going to do, Dale?'

'Malone knows where Julie is. I'm going to his apartment and make him tell.'

'He won't talk.'

'I've no scruples left, Georgia. I'll use their methods if I have to.'

'It's not in your nature, you're not like that.'

'I'll do it, just the same.'

She looked at me and said calmly: 'You won't need to. I know where she's gone. I heard them talking. She's at a house on East Seventy-second Street near the Cornell Medical College. It's called Greyling House.'

I said: 'Can I use your phone?'

'Of course.'

I made a call to the airport. There was

a flight to New York in ninety minutes. I put the receiver down and she said: 'You've plenty of time — I'll drive you out.'

'Thanks. What will you do now?'

'Stay on here. This is my home town. I must have been crazy to think of shooting Frank. Only I thought . . . ' She shrugged. 'I have friends here. I'll get over him now.' She fixed two more drinks and said: 'Good luck to you . . . Dale.'

'You've brought me the luck, Georgia. But for you I wouldn't know where to start looking.'

'She's beautiful, isn't she?'

'Yeah.'

'And you love her?'

'I'm fond of her. I'm not sure about love.'

'You mean in the sense of marrying?'

'I suppose that's what I mean. I don't think she wants marriage.'

'And you?'

'I don't know.'

'That means you aren't in love.' She eyed me candidly. 'Meeting you has done something for me. I don't know just how, but it has.'

'What?'

'I went to that place in a confused state of mind. You've straightened me out.'

'I'm glad.'

'I owe you a lot,' she said. She walked restlessly round the room. Then she turned slowly and came back and faced me. 'I like you,' she said simply.

I stood there, no more than inches from her. I hadn't been thinking of her in that way, but now I was. I forced myself to remember Julie Arden, but I couldn't stop the sudden unbidden leaping within me.

'I can give you something to remember me by,' she said.

I could see my hands shaking. I was hot and cold in alternating waves, possessed by a desire which a moment before hadn't even been there.

Then I heard a voice. It had to be my voice, though I scarcely knew it. A voice asking stupidly for another drink. She poured it. I put it down in a gulp and lit a cigarette at the second attempt. I had no notion of what to say next.

'You had quite a fight with yourself just then,' she said. 'I'm sorry you won it.'

She picked up her handbag and added: 'I'll drive you to the airport now.'

27

It was after three o'clock in the morning when the black and gold taxi turned under the 114-ft. overhang of the four-acre cantilevered roof of the Pan-Am Terminal Building, swung into the multi-lane approach road and sped down the Van Wyck Expressway into Manhattan. I stopped it at the intersection of Seventy-second and York Avenue and walked the rest of the way.

The house was in total darkness. A mongrel dog shuffled across the empty street and vanished down an entry. A small wind rose suddenly, slapping the torn page of a newspaper against my legs, and as suddenly died.

There was a picket fence in front of the house and a wide drive, unpaved. A big convertible, all violent red and flared fishtails, stood out on the drive. I went past it and down the side of the house, looking for a rear door. I found one round the back, facing a square of neatly-rolled lawn, and turned the lock back with the celluloid, but the door was bolted inside. I moved away, along the rear of the house, until I found a french window. There was a bolt on that, too.

I took my jacket off, wrapped it round a dislodged piece of crazy paving and broke a leaded pane. There was only a small crunch and the smashed glass fell on thick carpet. In another moment I had pulled the bolt up and was inside. I had no pencil-flash but the thin moonlight was enough to let me walk without knocking into furniture. I went across the room and into a hallway. The place was as quiet as a tomb. I hoped it wasn't going to be mine. I found the stairs and went up them on the balls of my feet, breathing through my mouth. The stairs came out on a wide landing with five doors. One of the doors had been left half-open and showed a bathroom. That left four bedrooms and she was in one of them, but which? I stood, not breathing now, listening.

Nothing.

I stood against one door after another until I had listened at three of them. There were human beings behind some of the doors, but they were sleeping without sound. The fourth door was smaller than the rest, recessed in a kind of alcove with an ottoman ranged against the wall.

Something stirred inside the room, a faint swish of sound, like restlessly moved bedclothes. Then a voice, a voice not speaking words. A voice making a small inarticulate sound.

Julie.

I turned the handle and leaned on the door. It didn't open. But it couldn't be bolted on the inside because they would want access to the room. I slid the wards back. They clicked faintly and the room went silent. She was probably rigid with fear. I pushed the door open and went in fast. I clapped a hand over her mouth as she opened it to scream.

In the dark room I was just a man, any man. I said: 'Julie — it's me. Dale.'

She was sitting up in bed. Her arms clutched at me. Her whole body was shaking.

'Don't try to speak,' I whispered. 'And don't make any sound that will carry. Just get your street clothes on.'

She nodded. I went back to the door and stood against it with my gun out. But they hadn't heard. I looked back. She was already dressed, her clothes shoved on. I put an arm round her shoulders and said: 'Have they done anything to you?'

'No.'

'If they had I'd have killed them,' I said.

'I'm all right, Dale. Except that . . . oh, God, I've been so terrified.'

'It's all over, Julie. We're going.' I started back across the floor with her, holding her to me. We were going through the door when a thought struck me. 'Wait — don't even move,' I said.

I took one of my cards out and went back into the bedroom and put it on the pillow.

We were at the base of the stairs when she said: 'What did you do when you went back?' The words were barely audible.

'I just want them to know who got you

out of here,' I said.

Three minutes later we were out of sight of the house. No taxi cruised past us, perhaps not surprisingly at this hour in a city where more than six hundred cabbies are mugged or beaten-up every year. We walked all the way to the quiet old midtown square where I lived. Nancy wasn't on duty at her little switchboard in the apartment house. Nobody was and maybe that was as well, too. We walked up the stairs to the place I call home, the one place in the world that has anything of the kind of man I am.

'I'll fix you a drink,' I said.

'Coffee, then.'

I nodded.

'If you'll show me your kitchenette I'll make it,' she said.

'No, you sit down.'

'All right, I . . . ' Suddenly and without warning, she went straight down on the floor. I picked her up and put her on the settee. Her eyes opened. 'My goodness, I fainted' she said. 'I never fainted before.'

'You've had a bad time, Julie, it's just delayed reaction.'

'I expect it is. I'll be all right now.'

'When you've had a long sleep. Perhaps you'd better have a stiff brandy and go to bed.'

'All right, then. Am I going to sleep with you?'

'Better not.'

She smiled. 'Why, don't you trust yourself?'

'Not in bed with you.'

'Perhaps I don't want you to.'

'Sleep is what you need,' I said. 'Now don't argue — get into bed.'

'Yes, Dr. Shand.' She walked, not quite steadily, into my bedroom and reappeared a few moments later wearing a suit of my pyjamas. They hung off her in long folds and made her look absurdly small, though she wasn't a small girl.

'Where are you going to pass the night, or what's left of it,' she demanded.

'On the settee. I've got spare blankets and things.'

'I'll make it up for you.'

'No, you won't. Off you go, and I'll bring the brandy.'

I made her a stiff drink and carried it in

317

and sat on the edge of the bed. After a little while she slid down, her hair spreading over the pillows. I kissed her forehead and turned out the lights and went swiftly from the bedroom while I still had the will-power.

*   *   *

The telephone rang at 9.20 a.m. I crawled off the settee and said something into it.

Nancy's surprised voice exclaimed: 'Why, hello, Mr. Shand — I didn't know you were back.'

'It was in the small hours, Nancy. I'm only half-awake.'

'Tck-tck,' said Nancy. 'You should arrange things so that you get a proper night's rest. Did you have an exciting trip?'

'You could say that . . . '

'All that lovely California sunshine. Some people are lucky.'

'Well, I'm glad to be back. What was it you wanted, Nancy?'

'I nearly forgot. I have a call for you.'

I yawned. 'Oh — who's calling?'

'Mr. John J. Fargerson — or, rather, his secretary.'

'You mean *the* Mr. Fargerson?'

'I don't know. I suppose so, unless this is another one. As a matter of fact, I told him you weren't in New York, but he insisted on my ringing you.'

'Better put him through, then,' I answered. I wondered what business John Justin Fargerson might have with me. All I knew about him was that he was a financier who had lately been in the headlines as an unexpected candidate for mayor. The general opinion was that he hadn't much of a chance — though Burr Allard, who is just about the best-informed newspaperman in New York, had told me that Fargerson might draw rather more water than some people imagined.

The call came through and a smooth, efficient voice said: 'Mr. Shand?'

'Speaking.'

'Mr. Fargerson's secretary. Mr. Fargerson would appreciate it if you would call on him at eleven this morning. He wishes to consult you professionally.'

'Can you give me any idea what it's about?'

'It's in connection with the mayoralty campaign. Certain unusual circumstances have arisen which are causing Mr. Fargerson some concern. I cannot be more precise than that. In any event, Mr. Fargerson would prefer to discuss the details with you in person.'

'At his campaign headquarters, you mean?'

'Mr. Fargerson suggests that a private consultation of this nature might be better conducted at his home. I take it you know the address.'

'As a matter of fact, no.'

'Number Four-A Carston Gardens, just off Central Park West.'

'At eleven o'clock?'

'Precisely at eleven. Mr. Fargerson is insistent on meticulous punctuality.'

'I'll be there,' I said. I went into my bedroom. Julie was still sleeping. I shaved, showered and put clothes on and called Burr Allard at his home. The bell rang for several moments before he answered. I guessed he had probably been sleeping too.

His deep, amiable voice said: 'I love being dragged out of bed at this hour after working till four in the morning. I suppose you want something?'

'Yes. What do you know about John Justin Fargerson?'

'Why?'

'His secretary just called me. It seems Fargerson wants to consult me.'

'That's interesting.'

'So I thought. Something about unusual circumstances having arisen. That could mean several things. Is he having trouble in his political campaign?'

'You mean is he being threatened or blackmailed?'

'Well, is he?'

'I never heard of anyone threatening to shoot him on the steps of City Hall,' answered Burr humorously. 'As to blackmail, so far as I know he leads a blameless life. On the other hand, how much does anybody know of a public man's private life?'

'There could be some hidden pressure.

He's rich, I take it?'

'That's the general impression, but I haven't seen his bank statement recently.'

'Don't be comic, Burr. What kind of man is he?'

'Tall, greying, well-built, wears the kind of suits I've never been able to afford. Lives well without yelling about it.'

'What's his business, in general terms?'

'President of Fargerson Finance Inc., offices on Pine Street near the Sixty Wall Tower. Believed to have made capital available for a number of private building projects, among other things. That's about all I know.'

'I never heard of him until recently,' I said. 'But, then, I don't get around much in big financial circles.'

'You probably wouldn't have heard of him at all if he hadn't decided to go into civic politics. In fact, nobody would. But as I told you previously, Fargerson is getting more support than some observers expected. He spreads money around where it makes friends.' Burr chuckled dryly. 'If he wants you to act for him in some capacity you ought to do well out of it. I hear he pays top money for service.'

'Well, money is a useful commodity.'

'If you get a fat fee you can buy me a dinner.'

'I'll do that. It's time we got together again.'

'That's right, it is. I never seem to hear from you nowadays unless you want something, shame on you. By the way, Fargerson's making a major campaign speech tonight. It's going out both on television and radio.'

'Oh?'

'Yes. His first broadcast. He's become important enough for the networks to notice him.'

'Thanks.' I hung up and stood looking at the cradled phone. Then I called Police Headquarters. Lou Magulies was in.

'So you're back in town,' he said.

'Yeah, I want to talk with you.'

'So do the cops out in L.A.'

'They're not after my blood, though.'

'No, but I've had Logan on the wire. You seem to have been causing them a whole lot of trouble.'

'Can I come down to Headquarters right away?'

'Sure, why not?'

'I'm bringing someone with me.'

'Oh?' His calm voice rose slightly.

'A Miss Julie Arden, who needs police protection.'

'Well, well,' said Magulies.

'I have to keep an appointment at eleven this morning. I'd like to feel that she was being looked after in my absence.'

'You mean she's in actual physical danger?'

'Yes.'

'All right, bring her,' he said.

I put the phone down and walked across to the window which overlooks the quiet square. A car was parked almost opposite. There was a man in it, a big shambling man in a grey suit. He was looking directly at the house. After a moment I heard the starter rasp. He drove the car, but not far — because the motor stopped. Dino Carelli was in New York and had found where I lived, which would be simple because my number is listed in the telephone book. The interesting thing was what he was waiting for. I thought I knew.

I went back into the bedroom. Julie was stirring. She sat up with a sudden smile. She looked much better. Thirty minutes later I parked my car and walked with her into Police Headquarters. Magulies was sitting behind his desk in the big detectives' room, still wearing the shiny blue suit he always wears, still looking relaxed and slow-moving, still probably the best captain of detectives this city has ever had. He stood up and gave Julie a hand.

'Dale wants us to kind of look after you, Miss Arden.' He smiled faintly. 'That's an unusual request to a department normally concerned only with homicide. However . . . ' He turned to me and said: 'Take a seat and start talking. If you want our help we want to know why — in triplicate, if need be.'

He listened in silence. When I had finished he said: 'I'll have some men go up to that house on Seventy-second Street, though I imagine the men who held Miss Arden there will have gone.'

'It's a certainty — just as the bunch who took me to the house in Beverly Hills did.'

Magulies spoke tersely into an intercom. Then he leaned back and said: 'Is it your theory that Fargerson is being threatened by The Organization?'

'I haven't yet made that suggestion. Maybe he'll tell me when we meet. What do you know about The Organization?'

'We know it's been in the process of formation as a new crime potential. We have reason to think that it is almost ready to act — probably in a dozen cities.'

'The man behind it used to be known as Johnny Cassatta.'

'Sure. Only nobody knows where he's got to.'

'He's almost certainly in New York.'

'I didn't mean that. Cassatta ceased to exist under that name a long time ago. If he is here it's as another and entirely different personality.'

'It doesn't help much, does it?' I said.

'It doesn't help at all. We don't *know* who we're looking for or where to start looking. He could be anybody. He could be squeezing Fargerson.' Magulies picked up a bank pen and turned it absently between his hands. 'Then there's Carelli,' he said gently. 'Maybe *he's* coming to New York, too.'

'He's already here. I saw him watching my apartment from a car not an hour ago. That's the last development . . . so far.'

Magulies put the pen down abruptly. 'You figure he thinks you might lead him to Cassatta?'

'It's possible. He may think O'Hara told me something, something I've kept back. In fact, he didn't because he never had the chance. But Carelli is desperate now. He'll try anything that looks like a lead.'

'But you don't know who Cassatta is any more than he does.'

'Carelli may think I do.'

'If he's tailing you that'll be exactly what he thinks. Did he follow you here?'

I nodded.

'We could pick him up for questioning,' mused Magulies. He eyed me directly.

'That wouldn't be much use, though, or would it?'

'No.' I stood up. 'I'll need to go if I'm to see Fargerson on time.'

'Yeah,' he said.

'And you'll take good care of Miss Arden?'

'Surely. You don't mind being with a bunch of rough coppers, do you, Miss Arden?'

'You look much nicer than that description, Captain Magulies,' murmured Julie.

Magulies grinned and glanced at me. 'Of course, if your appointment turns out to have anything to do with The Organization you'll have to tell us, Dale.'

'Of course. It might have.'

He gave me a long blank smile. 'That's why we're interested.'

'I thought you would be,' I said.

'On the other hand, it may not be necessary for you to tell us,' Magulies added softly.

His eyes held mine directly. I nodded and touched Julie's arm and went out and got into my car and drove north on

Lafayette through Union Square and north again on Broadway to Central Park West.

Dino Carelli picked me up on Lafayette and was behind me all the way.

28

It was a fine new house, all steel and dazzling white concrete, windows not more than sixty feet wide and a garage big enough for only a couple of Greyhound buses. There were two cars on the flagged driveway. One was a Rolls-Bentley. I put my four-year-old Buick convertible next to it and looked in the driving mirror. No sign of Carelli, but he wouldn't be far away.

I walked past the Rolls-Bentley and up six white steps into an arched porch and rang the bell. The door opened and a man in butler's uniform took my card with a fine disdain.

'If you will just wait inside a moment, sir . . . '

I waited inside, but not long. A slim, dark-suited young fellow with a long pale face came up the hallway.

'I'm Mr. Fargerson's secretary, we spoke together over the telephone.' He smiled. 'Please come this way, Mr. Shand.'

I followed him down about a quarter-mile of hallway floored with inlaid mosaic and dotted with elegant little side tables on curved legs and indoor-flowering plants in green-lacquered tubs bound with polished brass. There was a door at the end. He held it open for me and I went into a vast room furnished without regard to cost or taste. There was too much of everything — Chippendale and modern functional, blood-red mahogany and veneered walnut, a delicate Chinese carpet with violently-hued scatter rugs lazing on its surface like over-ripe islands, a television cabinet with a screen which looked wide enough for CinemaScope, and the obligatory bar — except that this one was a designer's misconception of an English inn.

Standing in the middle of about four thousand dollars' worth of carpet was a tall, greying man with a smooth, slightly over-fleshed face and warm brown eyes with a brilliant shine in them. He was wearing a flat blue suit of matchless cut and had his right hand in a jacket pocket.

'Mr. Fargerson?'

He nodded.

'I got your message,' I said.

He nodded again, his eyes on me in a long, slow look.

'Well, I'm here — exactly on time, Mr. Fargerson.'

He walked unhurriedly across the room to the phony English bar. He made two drinks without asking me what I would have and walked back and set the drinks down on a low side table. His lips moved. He was ready to speak.

'I'm so glad you were able to come, Mr. Shand,' he said.

The voice was a controlled voice, flat and almost devoid of expression; no longer amplified, no longer anonymous. A voice I had heard once and would always know again.

'You wished to consult me,' I said.

He smiled, but not with his eyes. There was nothing in his eyes. 'Consultation is not perhaps the exact word . . .'

'Maybe execution would be better . . . *amico*,' I said.

The brown eyes flickered. 'Yes, execution is the definitive word,' he purred. 'So you recognized my voice immediately, though when you entered here you could not have known that you were about to hear it.'

I didn't answer. He went on mockingly: 'It was so easy to bring you here, *amico*. I do not even have to send any of the trouble boys for you. Just a telephone message that the rich John Justin Fargerson is offering an assignment and you are here, sniffing fat rewards. They will, I fear, be less than agreeable.'

'Perhaps. On the other hand, it depends what you're bidding on.'

'A full house, Mr. Shand. Literally a full house, too . . . and you are in it. I need hardly say that the chances of your getting out of it alive do not exist.'

'You're making a campaign speech tonight,' I said. 'It was imperative that the only man outside The Organization who knows your voice shouldn't hear it. That about sums everything up, doesn't it?'

'Not quite everything. You will be required to tell us about Annette Falaise

— and a number of things concerning us with which you have foolishly meddled.' He took his hand out of his jacket pocket and said smilingly: 'I wasn't holding a gun. It will not be necessary.' He touched a small bell at the side of the enormous overmantel.

Frank Malone came swiftly into the room, his eyes glittering.

The tall greying man said urbanely: 'It will be Frank's task and pleasure to exercise his fullest ingenuity in the arts of persuasion, *amico*. I should explain that Frank is a sadist of immeasurable resource and wholly without human compassion. He and his assistants will shortly conduct you to the cellars. They are massively soundproofed — a very necessary precaution, since the devices they house are exquisitely fiendish.'

'You made one mistake, Fargerson,' I said.

A reflex twitched high up on his beautifully-shaven face. 'I never make mistakes, *amico* . . . I even tricked you into walking unawares into this trap.'

'That was the mistake, Fargerson or

Cassatta or whatever you choose to call yourself. You had your secretary call my apartment and insist on being put through to me, although the girl on the switchboard did not even know I was there. Nobody knew . . . *except you!*'

Malone said balefully: 'Let me work on him . . . '

Fargerson held up a ringed hand. 'In a moment. Go on, Mr. Shand.'

'I left my card in that house on Seventy-second Street. I left it deliberately. That was how you knew I was in New York. There was no other way. Whoever called my number insisting that I was there to take it *had* to be the man behind The Organization. It was as simple as that, and you fell for it.'

He wheeled on Malone. 'You've held something back!' he grated.

Malone's face was ashen. 'Haggart and Delmar told me when I arrived this morning that the girl must have managed to escape in some way on her own. They said they had heard Shand was back in New York . . . they said nothing about finding his card . . . ' He tongued his lips.

'I can figure why. They didn't want me to know Shand had walked right in under their noses and taken the girl out . . . '

Fargerson said dispassionately: 'Have them taken care of, Frank — very quickly. You will have to delay interrogating Shand.'

I laughed. 'The delay will be long, Fargerson. I've been to the police.'

Something sick looked out of his eyes. 'You have . . . *what*?' he whispered.

'The police know I'm here, Fargerson. Unless I misinterpreted the captain of detectives, this house will have a cordon round it by now. And there's something else.'

'Yes?' The flat voice was low, but back under control.

'Dino Carelli tailed me here. I guess he thought I knew something and might lead him where he wants to be. To you, Cassatta. He arrived just ahead of the police. I'd say he is here . . . inside this house.'

Malone jumped backwards against the wall. His right hand moved, very fast. But the door was already open and Dino

Carelli was standing in the opening . . . there was a shining blue streak in the air, then a scream from Malone as the long knife ripped through his forearm and pinned him to the wall.

'Knives is quieter, but I can use a gun, too, if I have to.' Carelli laughed, a thin rasp of sound. 'You've changed a lot, Johnny,' he said admiringly. 'I'd of passed you on the street without knowing — except for the voice. That's why you had to get me, why you had to get Shand as well.'

Fargerson said coolly: 'We don't have to fight, *amico*. A new deal all round. I'll cut you in on an equal partnership, straight down the middle, Dino.'

Carelli laughed again.

'No dice, Johnny, it's winner take all . . . I planned The Organization before I was sent up the river after *you* tipped the cops off. Yeah, I found out about that in the State pen. Well, you're all washed-up now, Johnny Cassatta Fargerson . . . ' A second knife jumped into his hand. He didn't even look at me.

'You're too late, Carelli,' I said. 'The

law is right behind you.'

Fargerson was already staring at the door. Magulies had come through it. He said: 'Put the knife up. There's a gun almost in your back.'

Carelli shrugged. There was a dull plop as the knife hit the floor.

For a long moment Fargerson stood utterly without movement, like a stone man. Then his mouth moved.

'Shand . . . ' He whispered the word. 'But for you everything would have been all right . . . ' His hand streaked inside his jacket, but I had already closed in on him. I hit him once, on the underside of his smooth jaw. His head snapped back, then he half staggered forward and pulled himself up.

'I guess that'll be about all,' said Magulies calmly. He made a faint grin, 'I said it might not be necessary for you to tell us what happened here, Dale.'

'Well, I took it to mean you'd be on hand,' I said. 'That and the look you gave me.'

'Yeah. I heard enough to hang charges on Fargerson. I dare say we'll uncover other things now.'

A young bluecoat unpinned Malone from the wall and started emergency first-aid.

Fargerson spilled brandy into a glass with shaking hands. 'You've nothing on me, captain,' he said.

'We'll see,' said Magulies impassively.

Fargerson sneered. 'I'll buy the best trial lawyer in New York,' he snapped.

'You'll need him,' answered Magulies.

29

It was a new place just off The Strip and up on the stand a girl in a white gown was singing the sophisticated disenchantment of Cole Porter — then some newer, specially-written material. She looked younger and slimmer than when we first met in a bar on a night which seemed to belong in another age.

'Annette looks wonderful,' Julie said softly.

'Better still, she's singing wonderfully.'

Julie squeezed my arm. 'And all because of you . . . '

'I told you she could be great again,' I said.

Annette came down off the stand and sat with us. She hardly looked like the same person. 'Bless you for everything,' she said.

'I'm getting too much flattery tonight,' I grinned.

She lit a cigarette and went on: 'What happened about Fargerson — or Cassatta?'

'The police found enough evidence in his house to smash The Organization. He had a complete file on every facet of their operations — key men, contacts, men who could be bribed, men who could be silenced, even the names of men who had been killed off.'

'And Dino?'

'He can plead self-defence for the shooting in that bar. I'd say he'll get off with manslaughter — though a smart attorney might conceivably get him a suspended sentence. If that happens he's going to the Argentine, I gather.'

For a moment she fell silent. Then she said: 'And The Organization is smashed, and but for you it would still be in existence. And you did all that for nothing!'

'I didn't have much choice, the way things broke. Besides, I've been paid.'

'Oh?'

'Not in money. In other ways. I've seen you come right back to the top. And I met Julie.'

She looked at me for a long unfathomable moment. 'Yes,' she said. She stubbed out her cigarette and added: 'I have to go back on the stand for the walk-down. I'll be free then. We'll all have supper together.'

'Sure.'

Julie said: 'She likes you. She'd be nice to you, if you wanted.'

'I never thought of her that way. She just meant something to me, something nostalgic about the way she used to sing.'

'You're just an old romantic, that's what.' She laughed. 'Not too old, though.'

'I just felt she could make it if she really tried.'

'Well, she has, and that's all on account of you, too. Everything's turned out right, like the happy ending in a story.'

'I thought the unhappy ending or even the non-ending was the in thing just now.'

'Don't be silly,' she said. 'Everybody loves a happy ending. It's so nice and cosy . . . and all because you chased girls across the United States. I suppose you're going back to New York,' she added inconsequently.

'Not just yet. We're going to have a vacation.'

'Oh, my — I've had enough travelling to last me for years.'

'We're going to see Sheriff Peel and Ma McGarritty,' I said.

'I still think you'd make a gorgeous deputy sheriff with a ten-gallon hat and two enormous guns in your belt.'

'I've thought about it, but I guess New York is where I belong.'

'I suppose so.' She looked up and said: 'I've had an offer from a big design house here in L.A. That's where I belong.'

'But not yet.'

'No,' she said, 'not yet.'

We went back to see Tom Peel and Ma McGarritty. Then we went south again, south of the border. We stayed three weeks. Three weeks I would remember the rest of my life.

It was warm and fragrant in Ensenada, with light breezes riffling down from the majestic peaks of the Sierra San Pedro Martir. A good spot to idle in with a pretty girl.

Except that we weren't idle . . .

We do hope that you have enjoyed reading this large print book.

Did you know that all of our titles are available for purchase?

We publish a wide range of high quality large print books including:
Romances, Mysteries, Classics
General Fiction
Non Fiction and Westerns

Special interest titles available in large print are:
The Little Oxford Dictionary
Music Book, Song Book
Hymn Book, Service Book

Also available from us courtesy of Oxford University Press:
Young Readers' Dictionary
(large print edition)
Young Readers' Thesaurus
(large print edition)

For further information or a free brochure, please contact us at:
Ulverscroft Large Print Books Ltd.,
The Green, Bradgate Road, Anstey,
Leicester, LE7 7FU, England.
Tel: (00 44) **0116 236 4325**
Fax: (00 44) **0116 234 0205**